THE MOST READ GUIDE IN HELL
FINALLY HERE, ON EARTH.
150
EXQUISITE HORROR BOOKS
Best Seller
GUIDA ESSENZIALE
AI MIGLIORI 150 LIBRI DELL'HORROR MODERNO
A CURA DEL PREMIO BRAM STOKER AWARD
ALESSANDRO MANZETTI

Join the Crystal Lake community today
on our newsletter and Patreon!

Interior Layout:
Lori Michelle—www.theauthorsalley.com

Hand drawn Illustrations by Stefano Cardoselli

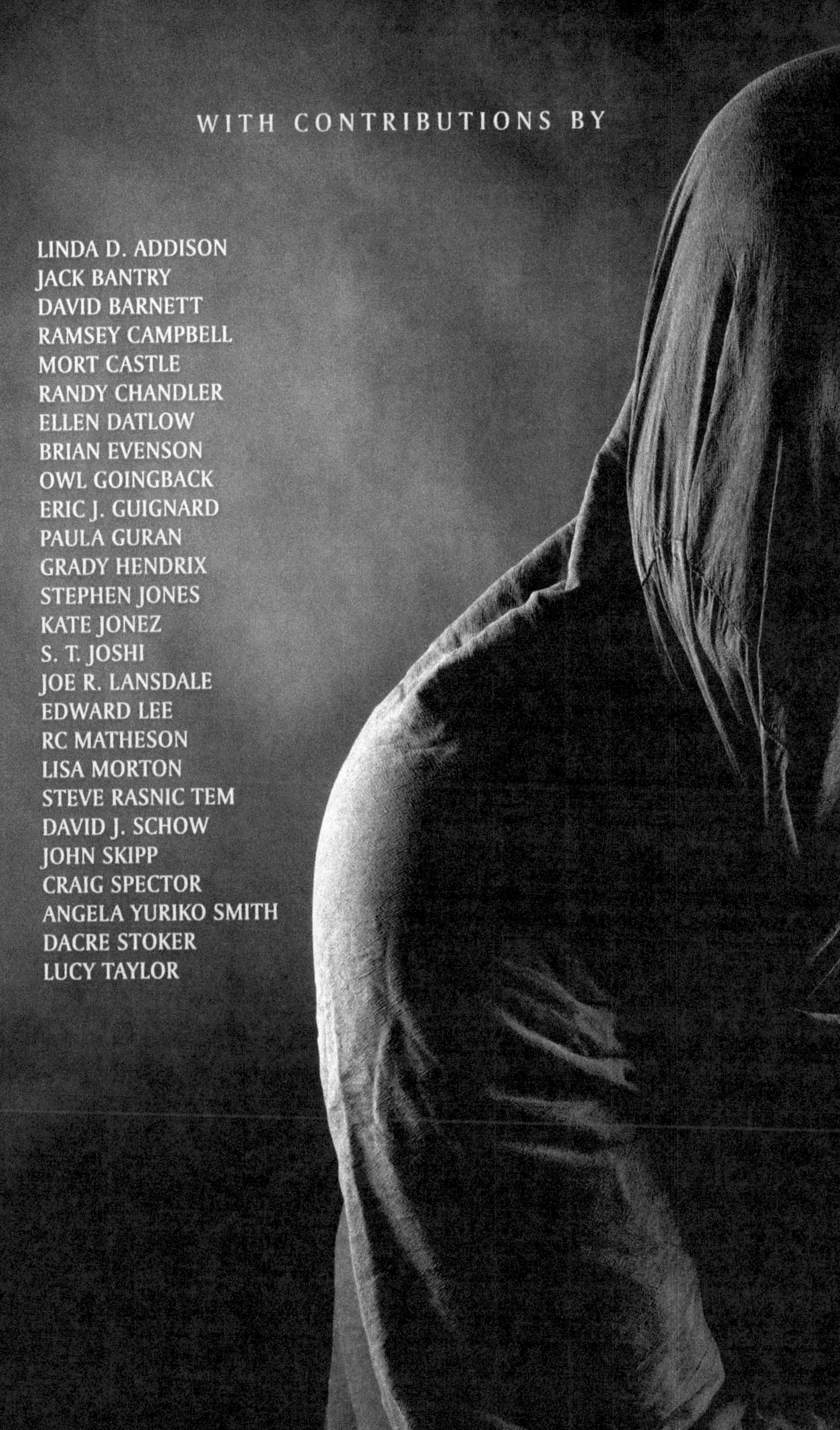

WITH CONTRIBUTIONS BY

LINDA D. ADDISON
JACK BANTRY
DAVID BARNETT
RAMSEY CAMPBELL
MORT CASTLE
RANDY CHANDLER
ELLEN DATLOW
BRIAN EVENSON
OWL GOINGBACK
ERIC J. GUIGNARD
PAULA GURAN
GRADY HENDRIX
STEPHEN JONES
KATE JONEZ
S. T. JOSHI
JOE R. LANSDALE
EDWARD LEE
RC MATHESON
LISA MORTON
STEVE RASNIC TEM
DAVID J. SCHOW
JOHN SKIPP
CRAIG SPECTOR
ANGELA YURIKO SMITH
DACRE STOKER
LUCY TAYLOR

WELCOME TO ANOTHER CRYSTAL LAKE PUBLISHING CREATION.

Thank you for supporting independent publishing and small presses. You rock, and hopefully you'll quickly realize why we've become one of the world's leading publishers of Dark Fiction and Horror. We have some of the world's best fans for a reason, and hopefully we'll be able to add you to that list really soon.

To follow us behind the scenes (while supporting independent publishing and our authors), be sure to join our interactive community of authors and readers on Patreon (https://www.patreon.com/CLP) for exclusive content. You can even subscribe to all our future releases. Otherwise drop by our website and online store (www.crystallakepub.com/). We'd love to have you.

**Welcome to Crystal Lake Publishing—
Tales from the Darkest Depths.**

AMAGO
OZZY
SC

A (Short) Introduction

By Alessandro Manzetti

THE PROJECT TO write a Guide to modern and contemporary horror literature dates back to 2014, and it took time to make it concrete in this volume, requiring many readings, studies and insights, and the support and continuous exchange of opinions from friends, authors, editors, critics, publishers and reviewers, some of whom are also among the contributors of this book.

This Guide selects works of horror, dark fantasy, weird and horror/thriller fiction, all originally published in English, from 1986 to 2020. I chose this period as 1986 marked a renewal in horror, followed by the coming of the early splatterpunk movement which brought to the fore new interpreters. These include Clive Barker, Joe R. Lansdale, Poppy Z. Brite, and many others who have profoundly changed the conceptual philosophy of dark and horror fiction. Furthermore, this period allows me to offer a particularly focused view on contemporary horror, covering books published in the last twenty years. Though, as you will see, the selection also touches on the late 80s and 90s.

Another aspect guiding this book and its selections is the definition of the genre itself. I have chosen to broaden this 'label' as much as possible to include—in addition to horror (and splatterpunk and hardcore/extreme horror)—other variations and subgenres such as dark fantasy, weird and thriller/horror works, putting them together in a so-called 'dark fiction' macro-genre. This variety of subgenres (and related influencing genres, notably SciFi) I think makes this guide interesting for different kinds of readers and fans, and does not exclude anyone.

In this Guide you will find a selection of 150 works of fiction, with a page dedicated to each book offering comments, my personal rating (using numerical marks expressed in hundredths) and the work's Goodreads score current at the time of writing. I have examined novels, short stories and short story collections, excluding anthologies, nonfiction, single stories and poetry collections. These will be addressed separately with the help of some specific and dedicated contributions. To broaden the proposal as much as possible, I have decided not to select more than three works per single author, allowing you a better chance of discovering as many interpreters of horror/dark fiction as possible.

The order of the works is alphabetical by the original English title. The scores I have assigned to each book are intended to represent my opinion in terms of the general quality of the works (which reviews, overall: style, content and originality), bearing in mind of course that all the books included herein are recommended by me. But I think it is important also to note the differences. I have tried to be objective—not putting into play my personal preferences or predilections in favour of particular subgenres or themes—but considering instead the whole spectrum of the dark fiction macro-genre offered on the market.

Since this guide is intended to be an 'essential' resource for readers and fans of the genre, not too many words are needed. You can easily find essays which delve deeper into single authors' works, genres, specific topics or themes. This Guide seeks to be something different, offering a new way of presenting horror and dark fiction for all readers, and not only for fans, field specialists and those working in the genre. I think we need to talk with a larger audience, allowing dark fiction to escape from the ghettos of its many small niches each with their own hidden pockets of readers. There are many potential fans out there who don't know enough to joins us, and we should try to involve them in a different, simpler way. To do that, we need first to light the fuse of their interest.

This short introduction must include a big thanks to the contributors who have enriched this volume, among them great authors, editors, essayists, critics and publishers who have each compiled their Top Ten different kinds of works (and some in-depth articles), offering readers accessible and user-friendly resources. Here are the contributors (in no particular order), among them many dear friends who supported this project: Lisa

Morton, Ellen Datlow, Eric J. Guignard, Craig Spector, Steve Rasnic Tem, Edward Lee, S.T. Joshi, Brian Evenson, Stephen Jones, Richard Christian Matheson, David J. Schow, Ramsey Campbell, Kate Jonez, Linda D. Addison, Paula Guran, David Barnett (who sadly passed away during the print of the Italian edition of the book), Joe R. Lansdale, Owl Goingback, John Skipp, Jack Bantry, Mort Castle, Randy Chandler, Grady Hendrix, Angela Yuriko Smith, Dacre Stoker and Lucy Taylor.

So, no more talking: it's time to discover the books I've selected for you, penned by authors who are proposing truly innovative and exciting stories, projects and ideas, allowing us to travel into a thousand fascinating worlds.

Happy exploring!

150 EXQUISITE HORROR BOOKS

EDITED BY ALESSANDRO MANZETTI

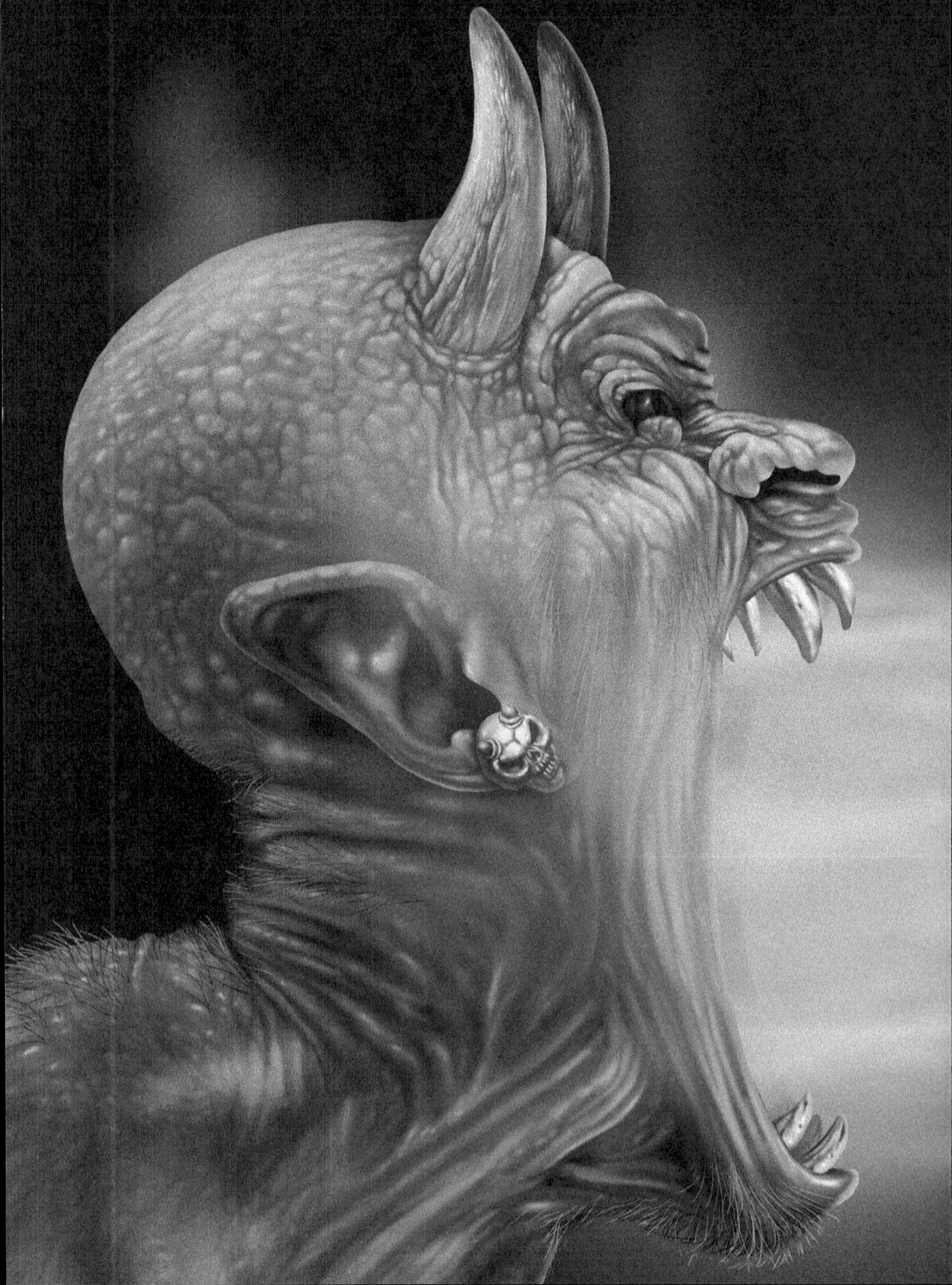

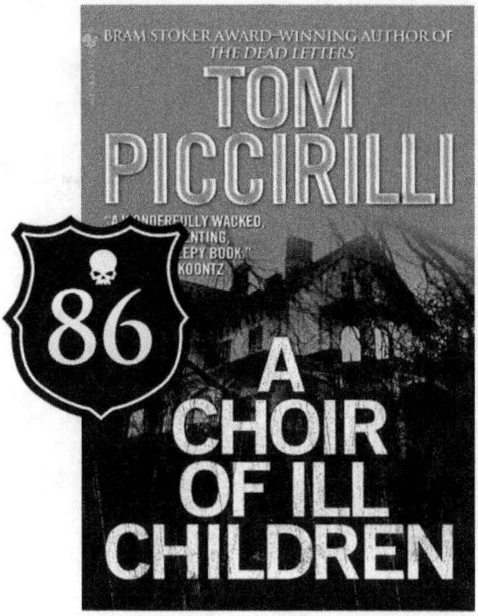

A CHOIR OF ILL CHILDREN

Author: **Tom Piccirilli**
Publisher: Bantam
Year of Publication: 2003
Genre: Horror
Typology: Novel
Total Score: 86
Goodreads Score: 3,68

Tom Piccirilli is an American author with many works spanning various genres to his credit. He has been successful in writing both fiction and poetry. His novel, *A Choir of Ill Children*, in my opinion represents his best work in the horror genre, both for the maturity of its style and the originality of its concept. This book stands out for its lyrical, dream-like quality. The events, located near a swamp in the town of Kingdom Come, mix sex, violence, ancient mysteries and madness. Following the disappearance of his parents, the protagonist, Thomas, must take care of both the family business (a mill) and his three brothers—Siamese twins who share the same brain while maintaining their own identities. But ancient horrors resurface from both the swamp and the past, presenting further tests for him under the burden of these challenges. Not a linear novel accessible to everyone, this work satisfies more complex palates.

A COLLAPSE OF HORSES

Author: **Brian Evenson**
Publisher: Coffee House
Year of Publication: 2016
Genre: Horror / Weird
Typology: Story Collection
Total Score: 90
Goodreads Score: 4,02

Brian Evenson is an exceptional writer, capable of wrangling offbeat fiction whilst maintaining a steady degree of excellence. Often compared to master storytellers such as Ballard, William S. Borroughs, Barthelme and Kafka, his contributions to horror and weird fiction are not to be missed. He knows how to capture his country, the United States, in a way few others dream of achieving. This collection of short stories, *A Collapse of Horses*, is I feel one of his best works in the horror/weird genre. This volume presents 17 unpredictable and surreal stories including murderous storms, ghostly visitors, horrific surgeries, hallucinations, organized cannibalism, and lurking presences, each of which engage the reader's perceptions. Evenson, fascinated by philosophy, proposes an obscure vision of the world and of death, attributing new meanings to the unknowable and the mysterious: these are the standard pieces he so deftly and skilfully moves across his literary chessboard.

A HEAD FULL OF GHOSTS

Author: **Paul Tremblay**
Publisher: William Morrow
Year of Publication: 2015
Genre: Horror
Typology: Novel
Total Score: 85
Goodreads Score: 3,80

Paul Tremblay is a top-class writer on the international market. The book I selected, his novel *A Head Full of Ghosts*, has earned him an even higher degree of respect. The life of the Barrett family is turned upside down by 14-year-old Marjorie, whose schizophrenia drags her into madness. Once it is understood that medical treatment is not able to help her, other solutions are sought—up to and including exorcism. The girl's father, unemployed and burdened with the expense of his daughter's therapies, is forced to open his troubled home to a reality television show, commodifying the shocking events unfolding in his family. This setup combines tragedy and spectacle: something very topical in today's world. The show proves to be a great success, and years later a journalist interviews Marjorie's sister to shed light on the behind-the-scenes goings-on of the controversial reality show. The story is told in an effective style, and offers an innovative take on the much-abused theme of possession.

A NEST OF NIGHTMARES

Author: **Lisa Tuttle**
Publisher: Sphere Books
Year of Publication: 1986
Genre: Horror / Weird
Typology: Story Collection
Total Score: 87
Goodreads Score: 3,91

Pain, guilt, loss, death. Lisa Tuttle, a very talented author, winds these dark threads through the 13 stories that make *A Nest of Nightmares*. This collection is one of the many examples of Tuttle's great contribution to the genre. Without making use of clichés and graphic content, the writer's psyche guides us through each story with subtle wisdom, compelling the reader to embrace the horror and restlessness therein, side-by-side with the main characters. Maybe it would be better to say 'female protagonists' than simply 'main characters', since this collection focuses on women, allowing us to test their loneliness, fear and uncertainty, character after character. A cross-section of the female world of the modern era, this work teeters on the edge of realities buffeted by deep, dark emotive waves.

ALL THE FABULOUS BEASTS

Author: **Priya Sharma**
Publisher: Undertow Publications
Year of Publication: 2018
Genre: Horror / Weird
Typology: Story Collection
Total Score: 89
Goodreads Score: 4,26

Another great author of the contemporary fantastic. In this collection of short stories, *All the Fabulous Beasts*, Priya Sharma pioneers an original interpretation of the genre, drawing on horror, the weird and the fairytale through effective, concise and engaging writing. We often talk about something 'new' in the field, and this author represents a real breath of fresh air. In this highly inspired collection, Sharma creates encounters with various fantastic human hybrids of birds, snakes, bees, and even ghosts. The powerful subtext flowing in the undercurrents of this volume is one of transformation through mutation. The contemporary fantastic and weird themes in this book often ally with magic realism, with excellent results.

ALONE WITH THE HORRORS

Author: **Ramsey Campbell**
Publisher: Arkham House
Year of Publication: 1993
Genre: Horror
Typology: Story Collection
Total Score: 90
Goodreads Score: 3,98

This volume collects many of the best short stories (totalling 39) by one of the great masters of horror, sampled from the years 1961 to 1991. Campbell's writing, with its peculiar literary style, shows all its nuances in this retrospective work. His unique interpretation of the genre is characterised by psychological distortion linked to the heritage of the Lovecraftian, and this flavor runs strong in Campbell's earlier works. This collection includes several well-known stories by the author, such as *The Companion*, *The Chimney*, *The Voice of the Beach*, *The Depths*, and *The Hands*. Campbell's works are not for everyone—even if greatly appreciated by aficionados of the genre—as they can be cryptic and elusive for casual readers. The most recent edition of this collection (Toe, 2005) includes a few more short stories.

BEST 10 HORROR BOOKS FROM 1986 TO 2020
SELECTED BY

GRADY HENDRIX

BLACK AMBROSIA by ELIZABETH ENGSTROM (1988)
BELOVED by TONI MORRISON (1987)
THE TOMMYKNOCKERS by STEPHEN KING (1987)
TOY CEMETERY by WILLIAM W. JOHNSTONE (1987)
LOST SOULS by POPPY Z. BRITE (1992)
X,Y by MICHAEL BLUMLEIN (1993)
UZUMAKI by JUNJI ITO (2000)
ROTTERS by DANIEL KRAUS (2011)
THROUGH THE WOODS by EMILY CARROLL (2014)
WHITE TEARS by HARI KUNZRU (2017)

GRADY HENDRIX is an American author, screenwriter, essayist and journalist. Among his works are: the novels *Horrorstör* (2014), *We Sold Our Souls* (2019), *The Southern Book Club's Guide to Slaying Vampires* (2020) and the essay *Paperbacks from Hell: The Twisted History of the 70s and 80s Horror Fiction* (2018).
Website: www.gradyhendrix.com

AMERICAN MORONS

Author: **Glen Hirshberg**
Publisher: Earthling Publications
Year of Publication: 2006
Genre: Horror / Mystery
Typology: Story Collection
Total Score: 85
Goodreads Score: 3,89

This is the second collection of short stories by an author able to satisfy the tastes of a wide audience, and not only those who are fans of the genre. Hirshberg's horror—which strikes subtly, and is never graphic—comes from everyday life as interpreted through well-rendered, vivid characters. This volume contains seven stories evoking a dark, mysterious, latent atmosphere which often leaves room for unexpected twists. Contemporary restlessness is well interpreted by the author, and the stories that best express his talent are *Safety Clowns*, *Flowers on their Bridles*, *Hooves in the Air* and the ghost story *The Muldoon*. Stephen King fans would likely appreciate Hirshberg's works, while those expecting action, gore, and more graphic content may find themselves a little disappointed.

ANIMALS

Author: **John Skipp & Craig Spector**
Publisher: Bantam Books
Year of Publication: 1993
Genre: Horror / Splatterpunk
Typology: Story Collection
Total Score: 87
Goodreads Score: 3,83

The latest novel by award-winning splatterpunk duo John Skipp and Craig Spector. If you love the werewolf subgenre, and you enjoy strong content with blood, violence and eroticism, this is the book for you. But beware, lycanthropy here is treated in a very original way. The explicit and graphic content peculiar to splatterpunk aside, this novel delves deeper into its characters than the duo's previous works have done, making this book unique to its peers in this particular subgenre. The collaborative works by these two heroes of splatterpunk (which are also well worth reading) are filled with a subversive charge which sparks with sharp, satirical criticisms of American society.

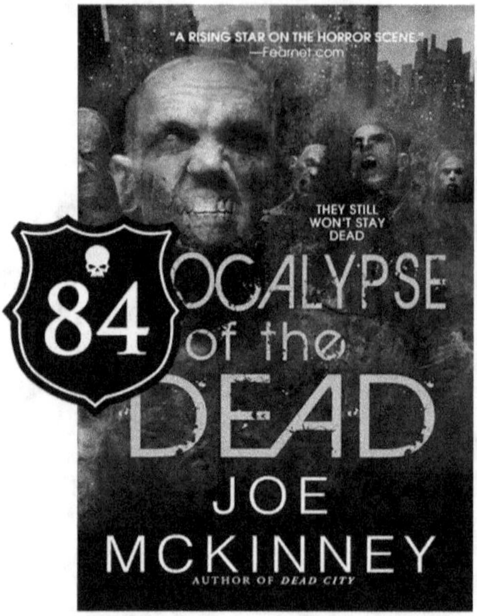

APOCALYPSE OF THE DEAD

Author: **Joe McKinney**
Publisher: Pinnacle
Year of Publication: 2010
Genre: Horror
Typology: Novel
Total Score: 84
Goodreads Score: 4,03

While I'm not a big fan of the zombie subgenre, some of its works deserve attention, and this is one of them. The second novel in the author's *Dead World* series, this title guarantees a fun and engaging read, thanks to McKinney's ability to build extremely vivid and enjoyable characters. The story covers a new epidemic which follows a series of hurricanes that hit the Gulf of Texas. The author allows us to track the fates of various groups of survivors, following a city in quarantine and a ship of refugees who roll the dice and sail away. But as expected, the infected are forever popping up all over the place. While this is the second instalment of a larger series, this novel can easily be read as a stand-alone in its own right. Recommended for fans of the zombie subgenre.

AT FEAR'S ALTAR

Author: **Richard Gavin**
Publisher: Hyppocampus
Year of Publication: 2012
Genre: Horror / Weird
Typology: Story Collection
Total Score: 88
Goodreads Score: 4,11

I could summarize this collection of short stories by Canadian author Richard Gavin simply as 'a weird gem'. These alchemical tales reveal a powerful imagination combined with a classic style, at times effectively recalling heterogeneous echoes of Stranzas, Machen, Lovecraft, Ligotti, Barron, and perhaps even Blackwood. This fusion of multiple visions makes Gavin's prose fascinating, elegant, evocative and modern, poising it on the edges of supernatural and cosmic horror. Among the most interesting and original stories collected in this volume are *The Abject*, *A Pallid Devil*, *Bearing Cypress*, *The Eldtritch Faith* and *Chapel in The Reeds*. But it's really hard to choose. This highly-recommended volume offers a real exploration into the most remote obscurities of the darker imagination.

BELOVED

Author: **Toni Morrison**
Publisher: Alfred A. Knopf
Year of Publication: 1987
Genre: Horror / Magic Realism
Typology: Novel
Total Score: 96
Goodreads Score: 3,89

A book with marked elements of magic realism in high-level literature, this Pulitzer-winning work blends a ghost story with brutal historical fiction depicting the lives of black people following the American Civil War. Toni Morrison is African American, and a winner of the Nobel Prize for Literature. Murder, sin, spirits and the psychological heritage of slavery are melded together in this work, giving life to a disturbing, deep, symbolic narrative. The author's dense, lyrical prose and unconventional narrative structure make this book a powerful conduit for deep emotions, even if not suited for quick or superficial reading. This novel is recommended for readers with more complex or refined literary tastes.

BIRD BOX

Author: **Josh Malerman**
Publisher: Ecco
Year of Publication: 2014
Genre: Horror / Thriller
Typology: Novel
Total Score: 84
Goodreads Score: 4,02

A well-known novel by now, thanks to the Netflix movie of the same name. Or rather the story is known, in a general sense, since the book obviously differs in part from the film adaptation even as the latter remains fairly faithful. The premise is original and engaging—which is surprising for an author's first novel—depicting the change of the status quo through the loss of the senses (in this case, sight). This story deftly navigates the horror, thriller and suspense genres, and immediately captivates the reader with its concept of mysterious creatures as the primary antagonists, the sight of which mean death for the surviving human beings. The author's style, while effective in the use of flashbacks and in the depiction of some scenes, misses something in the depiction of his characters and the credibility of some events—but the premise and concept remain fascinating, with a distinct Hitchcockian flavor.

BEST 10 HORROR BOOKS FROM 1986 TO 2020
SELECTED BY

RAMSEY CAMPBELL

REVIVAL by STEPHEN KING (2014)
THE LONEY by ANDREW MICHAEL HURLEY (2014)
DARK MATTER by MICHELLE PAVER (2010)
CUCKOO SONG by FRANCES HARDINGE (2014)
NO ONE GETS OUT ALIVE by ADAM NEVILL (2014)
DRAMAS FROM THE DEPTHS by REGGIE OLIVER (2010)
TWO WORLDS AND IN BETWEEN:
THE BEST OF CAITLÍN R. KIERNAN (VOL 1 and 2) by CAITLÍN R. KIERNAN (2011)
THE COLLECTED STRANGE STORIES OF ROBERT AICKMAN (VOL 1 and 2)
by ROBERT AICKMAN (1999)
20TH CENTURY GHOSTS by JOE HILL (2005)
A NEST OF NIGHTMARES by LISA TUTTLE (1986)

RAMSEY CAMPBELL is an English author, and one of the great masters of horror fiction. Among his works are the novels *The Doll Who Ate His Mother* (1976); *The Face That Must Die* (1979); *The Nameless* (1981); *The Hungry Moon* (1986); *Ancient Images* (1989); *The House on Nazareth Hill* (1996); *The Grin of the Dark* (2007); *Ghosts Know* (2011); *The Searching Dead* (2016); *The Wise Friend* (2020).

BLACK BUTTERFLIES

Author: **John Shirley**
Publisher: Leisure
Year of Publication: 1998
Genre: Horror / Dark Fantasy
Typology: Story Collection
Total Score: 87
Goodreads Score: 3,78

An author known for his cyberpunk and science fiction works, Shirley hides many other fascinating horror, dark fantasy and thriller works in his dark drawers. This award-winning collection of stories fully displays the author's gutsy and original style, made even more evident here in his short fiction works. Sex, drugs, street life, sexual abuse and perversion, alcoholism, death, and cannibalism are Shirley's chosen themes in these raw and disturbing stories. Divided into two sections: *This World* and *That World* (where the latter explicitly deals with supernatural scenarios), Shirley mixes multiple genres, including horror (including gore), dark fantasy and cyberpunk. These provocative and cutting stories guide the reader into the dark side extant in both the every day and the fantastic.

BLACK LEATHER REQUIRED

Author: **David J. Schow**
Publisher: Mark Z. Ziesing
Year of Publication: 1994
Genre: Horror/ Splatterpunk
Typology: Story Collection
Total Score: 90
Goodreads Score: 4,10

One of the most original and important collections of splatterpunk tales from a boundlessly talented author. I agree with John Farris' words in the Introduction, where he describes Schow as *'An urbanized Cormac McCarthy, but with a modern and malicious sense of humor'*. Death (and undeath) is the common thread in the stories Schow offers us here, a theme inhabited by robbers, junkies, bullies, drug dealers, monsters in disguise, and mutant alligators. The author's prose is of a high standard, sculpting characters and details complete with blemishes, and combining black humor, pulp, gore and surrealism to reveal an original interpretation of the horror genre. Among the most brilliant stories are *The Shaft* (which later became a novel), *Bad Guy Hats*, *Scoop Makes a Swirly* and a theatrical script that was supposed to bring the Grand Guignol back to Broadway.

BLACK WIND

Author: **F. Paul Wilson**
Publisher: Bookthrift Co
Year of Publication: 1988
Genre: Horror / Thriller
Typology: Novel
Total Score: 91
Goodreads Score: 4,27

A novel which combines the fantastic with historical reality—in this case World War II—and following real events such as Pearl Harbor, the Battle of the Midway, the Manhattan Project and, of course, the atomic attack on Japan. The plot outlines the comparison/clash between Japanese and American culture through four fascinating main characters. A mix of epic fiction, history and the supernatural develops the themes of good and evil, relationships between people, and intrigues and prejudices. Horror and fantasy elements are not explicitly displayed in this book, but rather subtly sketched. The path traced by Wilson in this book, which he himself considered his masterpiece, configures a compelling supernatural thriller with a historical theme.

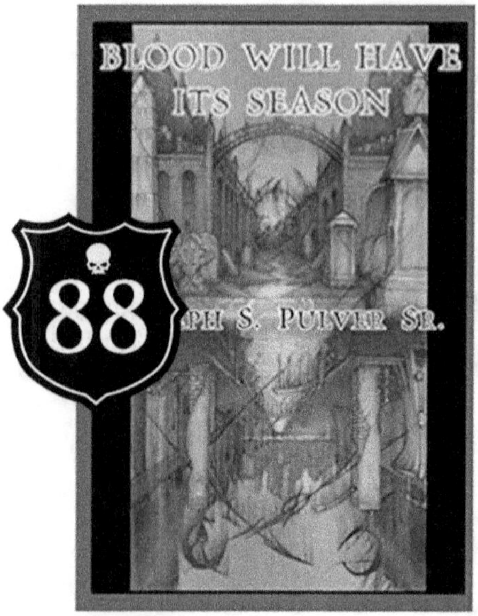

BLOOD WILL HAVE ITS SEASON

Author: **Joseph S. Pulver Sr.**
Publisher: Hippocampus
Year of Publication: 2009
Genre: Horror / Weird
Typology: Story Collection
Total Score : 88
Goodreads Score: 3,90

I have always been fascinated by Pulver's literary prose for its witchy poetry, and I consider him to be one of the most refined writers of the genre. The originality of his narrative vision is consistently well marked, even when incorporating the myths and elements of other authors such as Lovecraft and Chambers. Pulver's continuous experimentation leads him to present stories which often differ from each other in terms of theme, style and interpretation, but in the end—despite these differences and dichotomies—we always find ourselves in a sort of 'Pulver Universe'. Among the most intriguing stories included in this collection are *Yvrain's Black Dance* and *PITCH Nothing*. Defined by S.T. Joshi as a *'hypnotic collection'* (and this is precisely my impression, reading the book) and described by Thomas Ligotti as *'mortal and visionary prose, which makes you want to write the same things'*, Pulver's work (not just this book) represents a pinnacle of the modern weird.

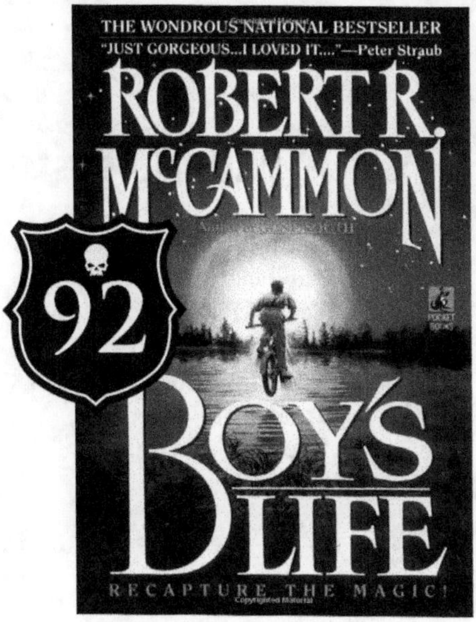

BOY'S LIFE

Author: **Robert R. McCammon**
Publisher: Open Road Media
Year of Publication: 1991
Genre: Horror
Typology: Novel
Total Score: 92
Goodreads Score: 4,36

One of the best coming-of-age horror novels, written by a great author. I would like to mention a comment author and editor Eric Guignard (and one of the contributors of this guide) made on this book, which I find really fitting: *'If you liked King's* The Body *(film adaptation:* Stand by Me*), in this book you will find a more exciting and deeper story, characterized by greater imagination'*. I add to these words that the author's style here truly is sparkling and effective, making perhaps McCammon's best work. The mood in these kinds of novels is always the same: the magical world surrounding us, which adults cannot see, revealing itself only to the eyes of children. Set in 1964, it follows the story of 12-year-old Cory in small town Alabama. The supernatural tints the story in a constant nostalgic undercurrent, highlighting the experience of the characters and the true magic and mystery of childhood.

BURNT BLACK SUNS

Author: **Simon Strantzas**
Publisher: Hippocampus
Year of Publication: 2014
Genre: Horror / Weird
Typology: Story Collection
Total Score: 86
Goodreads Score: 3,79

The fourth collection by this important author of the modern weird, worthy of some of the same remarks previously made on Pulver. This volume features nine short stories showcasing lyrical prose, each vivid and rich in the humanity of its characters without pandering to the reader—far from it. The themes explored in these stories include loss, insecurities, anxieties, and the changes in the world around us. The horror is tangible in all of these tales, with carefully-worked settings rich with an atmosphere that completely envelops the reader. Among the stories I preferred here are *On Ice* (an interesting interpretation of 'arctic horror'), *One Last Bloom* (the story of scientific research, in epistolary form), *Beyond the Banks* (originally written for a tribute anthology to *The King in Yellow* by Chambers), the hypnotic short story *Burnt Black Suns* (about the relationship between father and son) and *By Invisible Hands,* a tribute to Ligotti.

BEST 10 HORROR BOOKS FROM 1986 TO 2020
SELECTED BY

PAULA GURAN

PERFUME by PATRICK SÜSKIND (1985)
WALKING THE MOON by ELIZABETH HAND (1994)
BLACK BUFFERFLIES by JOHN SHIRLEY (1998)
THE GOOD HOUSE by TANANARIVE DUE (2003)
BEYOND BLACK by HILARY MANTEL (2005)
THE LITTLE STRANGER by SARAH WATERS (2009)
PORK PIE HAT by PETER STRAUB (1999)
THE KILLING MOON by N.K. JEMISIN (2012)
THE DROWNING GIRL by CAITLÍN R. KIERNAN (2012)
THE ONLY GOOD INDIANS by STEPHEN GRAHAM JONES (2020)

PAULA GURAN is an American editor, and is one of the most influential voices in the horror and dark fantasy field. She has edited more than 50 short story anthologies, including the well-known annual series *The Year's Best Dark Fantasy & Horror*. Guran also writes reviews, articles, interviews and columns for several magazines, including Locus Magazine, Publishers Weekly and Cemetery Dance Magazine. Website: www.paulaguran.com

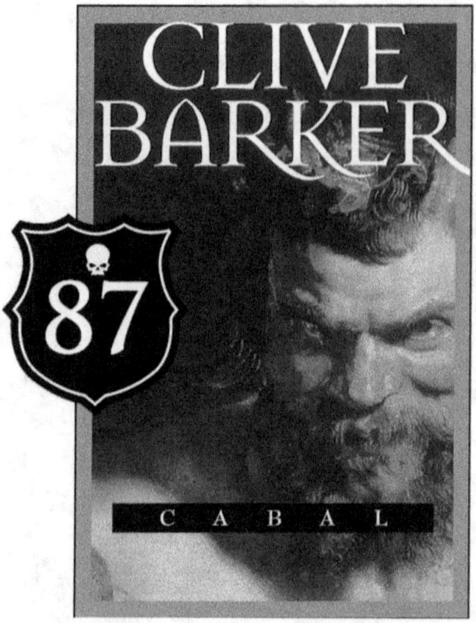

CABAL

Author: **Clive Barker**
Publisher: Gallery Books
Year of Publication: 1988
Genre: Horror / Dark Fantasy
Typology: Novel
Total Score: 87
Goodreads Score: 3,93

This work offers a brilliant example of fantastic fiction's ability to make itself an excellent carrier of complex metaphors concerning human existence. In this epic novel bridging horror and dark fantasy, Barker—through the monstrous inhabitants of the ghost town of Midian and its shape-shifters (Nightbreed)—subtly discusses discrimination against people, from homosexuals to those living in the ghettos, giving us various flavors of food for thought. A book should contain a message, and this book captures that ideal. A more superficial reading shows a truly enjoyable and highly engaging work. Barker's imagination, as evidenced in his other books, is superb, and the writing style never fails to deliver detailed, lyrical portraits. The main character, the troubled anti-hero Boone, deals with the real 'monster' of the book: the very human and perverse Dr Decker. This brilliant concept of an unconventional life framed as a 'monstrosity' to be persecuted, is alone enough to recommend this novel.

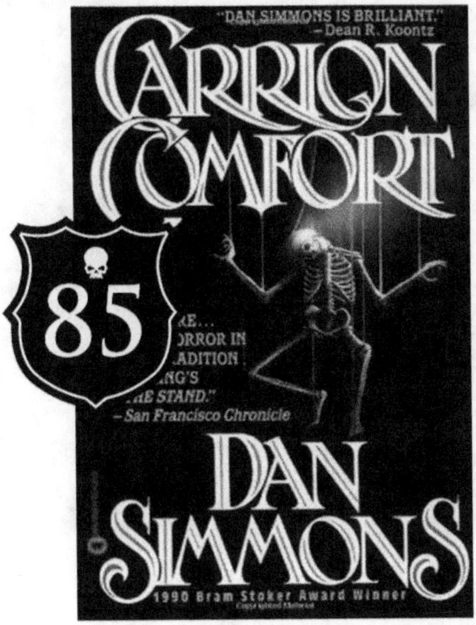

CARRION COMFORT

Author: **Dan Simmons**
Publisher: Warner Books
Year of Publication: 1990
Genre: Horror / Thriller
Typology: Novel
Total Score: 85
Goodreads Score: 3,90

A heavy (in terms of length, but not only) book by Simmons, this work proposes interesting themes in addition to the obvious in-depth analysis of Nazi concentration camps, such as control over the mind, fanaticism of power and the corruption of the human soul. Here horror elements are artfully wedged into a story full of suspense and action. Events kick off during World War II with the main character, Saul Laski, imprisoned in the Chelmno extermination camp, and reach the end of the '80s in Charleston where we are introduced to Willi, Nina and Melanie. These 'mental vampires' (Simmons defines them as such) are members of a secret society seemingly behind the most horrifying events in human history. The main characters are successfully rendered, and the structure of this chess game (a metaphor not casually used in this description) between hunters and prey works well despite the (perhaps excessive) length of the novel. A highly effective horror story cut to the pattern of a thriller.

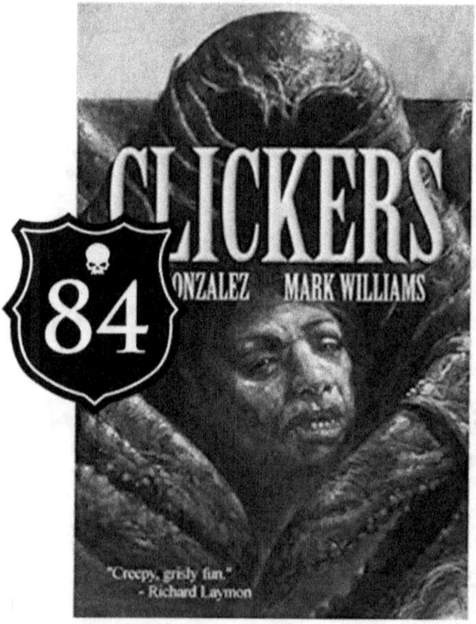

CLICKERS

Author: **J.F. Gonzalez and M. Williams**
Publisher: Delirium Books
Year of Publication: 1999
Genre: Horror / Extreme Horror
Typology: Novel
Total Score: 84
Goodreads Score: 3,84

Many define this work as a pulp novel, a B-Movie in book format, and I can agree. For fans of the genre, *Clickers* is like going to the carnival. The story starts strong, in the quiet town of Phillipsport, Maine, where hundreds of threatening killer creatures begin to emerge from the ocean. These are the *Clickers*: large poisonous crabs from the deep sea. The battle of the human species against these invaders immediately becomes mad and bloody. But just when everything seems clear, the poor residents of Phillisport are targeted by an even more dangerous predator—something those damn killer crabs were running away from. Written in a frenzied rhythm, this very enjoyable and creative work makes the first chapter in the series of the same name (other volumes have been written together with Brian Keene).

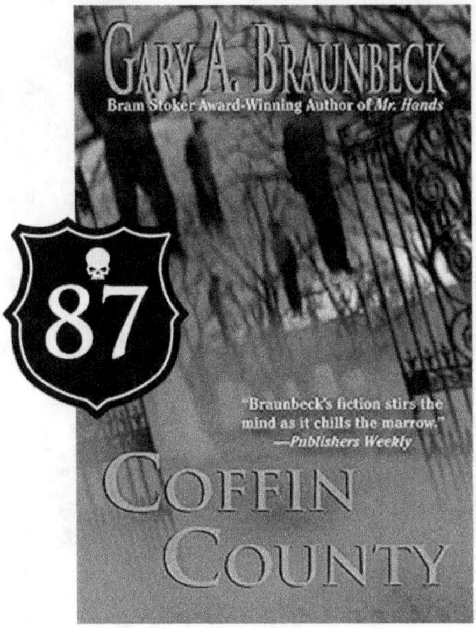

COFFIN COUNTY

Author: **Gary A. Braunbeck**
Publisher: Leisure Books
Year of Publication: 2008
Genre: Horror
Typology: Novel
Total Score: 87
Goodreads Score: 3,67

Cedar Hill is the imaginary hunting ground in which Braunbeck—with his refined pen—sets many of his stories, including this one. A town already marked by blood during its colonization two centuries ago, here a series of heinous murders open the hunt for a killer. But a Midwestern town, a serial killer, the supernatural or an abandoned cemetery alone do not make a novel—or better, these alone are certainly not enough for an author of Braunbeck's calibre. After the chaos of the first part of the book—where various gruesome events are chronicled—and over a wider span of time, Braunbeck begins to reveal his plan, going to the roots of violence and human restlessness in a clean, sparkling writing style. A curse, a reverend, a policeman, a city upset by the unknown—this is a hellish journey which, like all of this author's books, cannot be explained but must instead be experienced page by page.

COME CLOSER

Author: **Sara Gran**
Publisher: Soho Press
Year of Publication: 2003
Genre: Horror / Thriller
Typology: Novel
Total Score: 83
Goodreads Score: 3,60

This agile novel tells the story of Amanda, and her slip from a supposedly normal life into a nightmare. Strange noises in the apartment, bizarre events, something hidden in the shadows—or perhaps inside herself. No rational—much less medical—explanation is offered. How far is madness from possession, or from happiness? And how much does possession have to do with the desire for freedom, or with obsessions? Halfway between horror and psychological thriller, in this book Sara Gran tries to answer these questions, shedding light on the human personality and its hidden intrigues through engaging and compelling first-person prose best suited for the themes and vibe of this story.

COME FYGURES COME SHADOWES

Author: **Richard Matheson**
Publisher: Gauntlet Press
Year of Publication: 2003
Genre: Horror
Typology: Novella
Total Score: 87
Goodreads Score: 4.15

Here I make an exception to my criteria by selecting an unfinished work—one which should have become a novel, but never did. I think this could be an interesting discovery for fans, and an author like Richard Matheson makes it well worth the venture. Set in Brooklyn in the 1930s, this book tells the story of 18-year-old Claire, destined to follow in the footsteps of her fanatical mother, Morna, who is a medium. Here we are offered a fascinating and detailed picture of Spiritism in the period before World War II, exquisitely detailed by the author's careful historical research on this subject. In his Afterword, Matheson discusses what this unfinished novel should have become, which was originally expected to reach over two thousand pages. Due to the lack of interest by publishers in such a long work, it was abandoned in a drawer and never saw completion.

BEST 10 HORROR BOOKS FROM 1986 TO 2020
SELECTED BY

S.T. JOSHI

THE COLOR OVER OCCAM by JONATHAN THOMAS (2012)
PHANTOM EFFECT by MICHAEL ARONOVITZ (2016)
EXPERIMENTAL FILM by GEMMA FILES (2015)
THE RED TREE by CAITLÍN R. KIERNAN (2009)
HOUSE OF WINDOWS by JOHN LANGAN (2009)
BURNT BLACK SUNS by SIMON STRANTZAS (2014)
THE HOUSE ON NAZARETH HILL by RAMSEY CAMPBELL (1996)
GRIMSCRIBE: HIS LIVES AND WORKS by THOMAS LIGOTTI (1991)
SLIPPIN' INTO DARKNESS by NORMAN PARTRIDGE (1994)
A DARK MATTER by PETER STRAUB (2010)

S.T. Joshi is an American writer, critic, editor and essayist whose work has largely centered on weird and fantastic fiction, with a particular focus on the life and works of H.P. Lovecraft. His non-fiction publications include: *John Dickson Carr: A Critical Study* (1990); *The Weird Tale* (1990); *Lord Dunsany: Master of the Anglo-Irish Imagination* (1995); *HP Lovecraft: A Life* (1996); *Sixty Years of Arkham House: A History and Bibliography* (1999); *The Rise and Fall of the Cthulhu Mythos* (2008); *I Am Providence: The Life and Times of H.P. Lovecraft* (2 vol. 2010). Website: http://stjoshi.org/

COYOTE SONGS

Author: **Gabino Iglesias**
Publisher: Broken River Books
Year of Publication: 2018
Genre: Horror / Magic Realism / Horror
Typology: Novel
Total Score: 93
Goodreads Score: 4.30

A novel with a peculiar structure, composed of various stories and different characters who live near the border between the United States and Mexico. Told from multiple perspectives, Pedrito the coyote, Alma, La Bruja and Mister Iglesias are some of the voices giving life and breath to this book in a stimulating mix of genres which include horror, magic realism and psychological thriller. A powerful journey into Mexican culture, stepping between superstitions and illegal immigration, here the characters live in full breadth, experiencing pains, joys (few), poverty and crime. This tapestry of immigration tales is woven from all the dark 'songs' that speak of love, hate, injustice and torment, concerning both human and supernatural spirits. Each story works to form a vivid mosaic, creating a collection drenched in magic. 'Coyote' is a term for people involved in human trafficking between the US border and Mexico.

CROTA

Author: **Owl Goingback**
Publisher: Signet
Year of Publication: 1996
Genre: Horror / Dark Fantasy / Thriller
Typology: Novel
Total Score: 86
Goodreads Score: 3,88

Owl Goingback is a born storyteller, and if we combine this ability with his direct knowledge of Native American folklore (he is a descendant of the Choctaw-Cherokee people) the result can only be fascinating. This is the case here in his best-known novel, *Crota*, where an ancestral killer creature (trapped in a cave a long time ago by shamanic spells) manages to break free and wreak havoc upon the world. A trail of blood and slaughter in Hobbs County draws us into the story, where we are lead by the two main characters: Sheriff Skipp Harding and the young Native American Jay Little Hawk. There is no slacking off in the 'crime' element of this novel, taking it beyond the horror genre by mixing it in with thriller and dark fantasy. The author's style is clean and effective, and this book can be appreciated by a wide audience—including those generally disinterested in the genre.

DARK DANCE

Author: **Tanith Lee**
Publisher: Dell
Year of Publication: 1992
Genre: Horror
Typology: Novel
Total Score: 83
Goodreads Score: 3,74

A vampire story penned by of one of the subgenre's most brilliant interpreters, who unfortunately passed away in 2015. The protagonist, Rachaela Day, is an ordinary woman born to absent and indifferent parents, living alone and working in a bookshop in London. Her simple life is disrupted when the family of her ever-absent father turns out to be a sort of vampire clan. She is asked to come back and stay with them and, following some resistance, Rachaela ends up in the middle of nowhere in a manor on a moor. She is trapped—and she is not alone. Lee's prose is always of a high standard, and in this book she creates a strong, claustrophobic atmosphere mixed with a dark sensuality which might even be described as deviant. This is an original, neo-Gothic interpretation of the vampire subgenre.

DEAD IN THE WEST

Author: **Joe R. Lansdale**
Publisher: Night Shade
Year of Publication: 1986
Genre: Horror / Weird / Western
Typology: Novel
Total Score: 91
Goodreads Score: 3,84

Mud Creek, Texas is under a curse cast by a traveling Indian medicine man who sold tonics and lucky charms before being lynched, along with his wife, by the town's citizens. Now when darkness falls the undead walk the streets, hungry for human flesh. The novel's main character and perfect anti-hero is the Reverend Jebediah Mercer, who believes in his whiskey more than his God, arriving in Mud Creek during a zombie apocalypse led by our shaman in demonic form. Lansdale's style is inimitable, and makes this novel—a tribute to the pulp magazines of the past—fun and fresh despite the lack of innovation in the zombie theme. But the author, thanks to his talent, manages to keep readers clinging to the story and its cleverly-drawn characters without sticking solely to the shootings, killings and other pulp elements that ooze from the book. A cult classic for fans of the genre.

DEAD OF NIGHT

Author: **Jonathan Maberry**
Publisher: St. Martin's Griffin
Year of Publication: 2011
Genre: Horror
Typology: Novel
Total Score: 84
Goodreads Score: 3,97

Another zombie-themed novel by one of the best interpreters of this subgenre, Jonathan Maberry. Stebbins County, Pennsylvania. Homer Gibbo, a well-known serial killer on death row, is executed by lethal injection. The story begins at this event. The substance which the prison doctor injects into the man's blood is a formula designed to keep consciousness alive and clear even after the body dies. Certainly our serial killer will not rest peacefully in the grave, that's certain—and this doesn't just apply to him alone. Maberry's zombies feature innovations which break away from the usual clichés: they are aware of their gruesome actions (even if they have no control over them), and they are able to spitting out a disgusting contagious substance. Their 'intelligent' point of view and the scientific basis supporting the contagion are the strengths of this book.

DEPRAVED

Author: **Bryan Smith**
Publisher: Leisure
Year of Publication: 2009
Genre: Horror / Slasher / Hardcore Horror
Typology: Novel
Total Score: 82
Goodreads Score: 3,80

You'll find accents reminiscent of Richard Laymon and Edward Lee in this strong slasher horror novel showcasing grotesque violence, graphic sex, humor, blood and guts. In my opinion, this book is Bryan Smith's best work so far. Some readers will recognize elements taken from Rob Zombie or *The Texas Chainsaw Massacre*, but there is much more to enjoy here of its own unique flavor. A crazy vision of hell on earth, the story moves at a frenzied pace, confronting the reader with cannibals and deformed, mutant psychopaths. The story, described cinematically, is set in Hopkins Bend. This remote town in Tennessee hides a secret curse where the inhabitants are cannibals, and where sex trafficking is managed by local law. Given the strong violent content (there is no lack of incest, rape and other atrocities), this book is not for everyone—but it's a great gold nugget for the fans of the genre.

BEST 10 HARDCORE HORROR BOOKS FROM 1986 TO 2020
SELECTED BY

EDWARD LEE

THE GIRL NEXT DOOR by JACK KETCHUM (1989)
SLOB by REX MILLER (1987)
FRENZY by REX MILLER (1988)
THE BEAST HOUSE by RICHARD LAYMON (1986)
GHOUL by MICHAEL SLADE (1987)
DREAD IN THE BEAST by CHARLEE JACOB (1998)
GENITAL GRINDER by RYAN HARDING (2012)
POISONING EROS by WRATH JAMES WHITE & MONICA J. O'ROURKE (2002)
SURVIVOR by J. F. GONZALEZ (2004)
DUET FOR THE DEVIL by T. WINTER-DAMON & R. CHANDLER (2000)

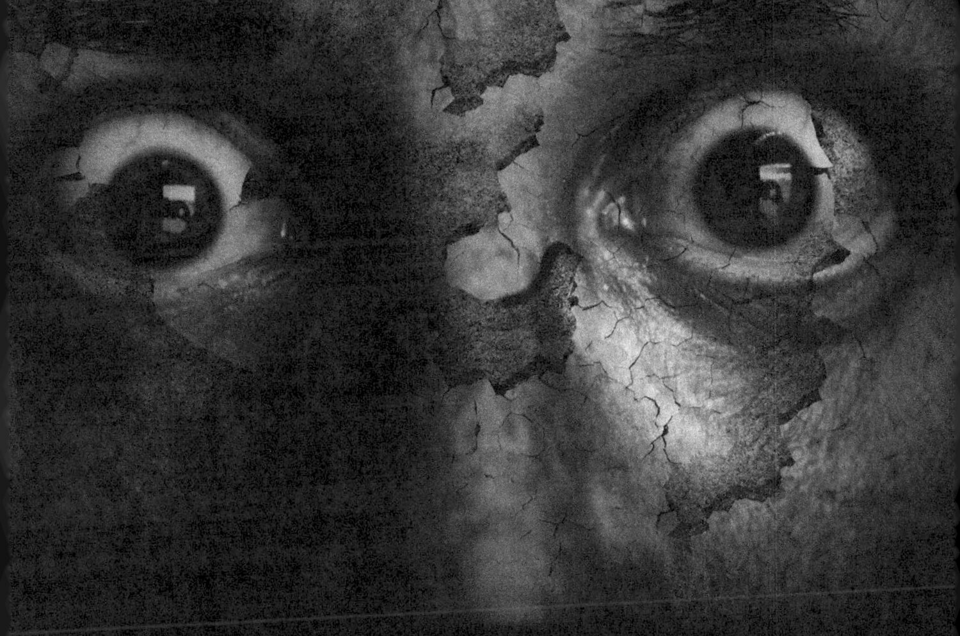

EDWARD LEE is an American writer, most notably recognized as a key contributor to the hardcore/extreme horror genre. His works include *Header* (1995), *The Bighead* (1997), *City Infernal* (2001), *Monstrosity* (2002),*The Backwoods* (2005), *The Minotauress* (2008), *Header 2* (2010), *White Trash Gothic* (2017) and *In the Year of Our Lord* (2019).

DOCTOR SLEEP

Author: **Stephen King**
Publisher: Scribner
Year of Publication: 2013
Genre: Horror
Typology: Novel
Total Score: 89
Goodreads Score: 4,11

Stephen King's return to the past characters and locations (including the famous Overlook Hotel) of one of his most successful novels, *The Shining*. Danny Torrance—the iconic child protagonist of the previous novel—returns, without his tricycle this time, as a full-grown man complete with his own problems. A nomadic tribe called The True Knot, led by Rose the Hat, travels America feeding on the 'steam' of their victims—this 'steam' is the vital essence of children with psychic abilities (children who 'shine'). Torrance's demons have continued to haunt him into adulthood, but his psychic gift of 'shining' resurfaces after he forms a bond with 12-year-old Abra. This fateful meeting will make all the difference in this clash between good and evil. This novel certainly cannot be compared with *The Shining*—which remains one of King's masterpieces—but we are given an excellent work which deals with themes such as addiction (alcoholism and 'steam') and redemption. The novel doesn't disappoint as the sequel to a work which made horror history (also thanks to Kubrick's movie adaptation and 'reinterpretation', which King famously resented for a time)—and that's no small feat.

DRAWING BLOOD

Author: **Poppy Z. Brite**
Publisher: Dell
Year of Publication: 1993
Genre: Horror
Typology: Novel
Total Score: 92
Goodreads Score: 4,03

The second novel by Poppy Z. Brite (now Billy Martin)—a big name in modern dark fiction—characterizes the author's writing even more than the better-known book *Exquisite Corpse*. As a child, Trevor McGee wakes to find that his father, a well-known cartoonist, has killed his mother and younger brother and then hanged himself. Twenty years later, Trevor—who has become a cartoonist like his father—returns to the town of Missing Mile, and to the house where his family was exterminated, looking for answers. Namely, why did his father spare his life? Alongside the main protagonist comes a second key character: 19-year-old hacker Zachary, who likewise lives under the torment of a rough childhood. The two fall in love and, through the use of hallucinogenic substances, Trevor manages to access the secrets of his past—which he does by entering a parallel reality called Birdland. The spirit of youth and homosexuality are told in Brite's decadent, lyrical prose, accompanied by the notes of Charlie Parker.

DREAD IN THE BEAST

Author: **Charlee Jacob**
Publisher: Necro Publications
Year of Publication: 1998
Genre: Hardcore Horror / Extreme Horror
Typology: Novel
Total Score: 95
Goodreads Score: 3,95

I agree with the opinion of Edward Lee, who in his Introduction credits this book as 'one of (his) favorite genre novels of all time'. The imaginary worlds Jacob crafts (disruptive and extreme) are beautifully carved by a grandiose, lyrical, acid and modern prose which stands among the best of the genre. This visionary novel was born from a story of the same title originally included in a previous collection. In this longer work, the author develops the theme of ancient and forbidden divinities. Inspired by human mythology and running in balance between the sublime and the profane, holiness and blasphemy, sex and death, Jacob fearlessly paints the worst human obsessions and deviations in vivid colors. From the sewers of Rome to cosmic baths and into the contemporary world, the dystopian myth of Jacob's 'Goddess' whips the reader through a whirlwind of emotions and sensations, sparing nothing. Given its strong content, this is only for firm fans of the genre.

DWELLER

Author: **Jeff Strand**
Publisher: Leisure
Year of Publication: 2010
Genre: Horror
Typology: Novel
Total Score: 84
Goodreads Score: 3,97

No doubt my favorite work by this author. An engaging and exciting novel that tells the story of an unlikely friendship between the protagonist, Toby, and a Bigfoot-like creature. They first meet in Toby's childhood, when he comes across the creature in a cave in the woods. Toby's parents convince him that the encounter was just his imagination—but the boy meets the creature again as a teenager, and a bond is formed. Toby feels safe with his friend, away from school bullies and the other torments that make his daily life. The monster likewise cares for Toby, and their strange friendship continues across many years, running parallel to the courses of their lives—with a few surprising twists. As with Strand's other works, action, blood and fun are never lacking, but this well-written book is particularly touching.

EVERYTHING YOU NEED

Author: **Michael Marshall Smith**
Publisher: Earthling
Year of Publication: 2013
Genre: Horror / Dark Fantasy / Weird
Typology: Story Collection
Total Score: 86
Goodreads Score: 4,21

A collection of 17 short stories covering various genres—from horror to dark fantasy, from weird to science fiction—making for a compelling introduction to the 'fantastic' through the mind of a very talented author. Smith manages to form dark pearls from small fragments of everyday life. These obscure jewels embed the author's view of reality and imagination, shining brightly in his fiction. The author is a remarkable interpreter of the genre, presenting stories which often feel like sharp, vivid, short movies. My favorite tales from this fascinating collection include *Walking Wounded*, *The Woodcutter*, *Unbelief* and *The Stuff That Goes on in Their Heads.*

EXPERIMENTAL FILM

Author: **Gemma Files**
Publisher: ChiZine
Year of Publication: 2015
Genre: Horror
Typology: Novel
Total Score: 88
Goodreads Score: 3,62

A modern ghost story with roots planted in cosmic horror. This complex tale taps into hidden emotions and, by avoiding the more direct narrative approaches, manages to go beyond the genre, ranging across several themes and mediums including cinematography, writing and visual art. The story follows film history teacher Lois Cairns as she obsesses over documenting the life of a late twentieth-century experimental director from Canada who has since disappeared. Her investigation of an old motion picture awakens the ghosts of the past—and the ghosts of beyond. Written like a memoir, this is a compelling and suspenseful read. Files' linear writing style is very effective for the purposes of this novel.

BEST 10 HORROR STORIES
SELECTED AND COMMENTED BY

STEPHEN JONES

My Top Ten Horror Stories

BY STEPHEN JONES

I suspect like many other writers and editors in my genre, I sometimes lay awake at night constructing the perfect horror anthology in my mind. Compiling a good anthology is no easy thing. An editor has to worry not only about which authors and which stories to select, but also how to put the book together so that the stories flow—for example, you don't want two stories with similar themes next to each other, and you need to vary the word-lengths and styles so that you retain the reader's interest throughout. Here are ten very different terrors that I would have no hesitation recommending to anyone interested in discovering the diversity of the horror genre

A Warning to the Curious by M.R. James. No horror anthology would be complete without a contribution by M. (Montague) R. (Rhodes) James (1862–1936), that English master of supernatural fiction. The Cambridge Provost invented the modern ghost story as we know it, replacing the Gothic horrors of the previous century with more contemporary settings and subtle terrors. Although his tales have been much imitated, they have never been surpassed, and among the very best is 'A Warning to the Curious' which, with its cursed object and doomed protagonist, perfectly exemplifies everything that is memorable about the author's fiction. I was proud to compile *Curious Warnings: The Great Ghost Stories of M.R. James,* a definitive collection of James' fiction beautifully illustrated by Les Edwards, for Jo Fletcher Books several years ago.

The Call of Cthulhu by H.P. Lovecraft. Next comes that dean of cosmic horror, H. (Howard) P. (Phillips) Lovecraft (1890–1937). A life-long antiquarian and resident of Providence, Rhode Island, most of his work appeared in the cheaply produced pulp magazines that he despised. He's best remembered for his creation of the much-imitated Cthulhu Mythos, his tales of ancient and unimaginable creatures seeking to reclaim the Earth; they are as powerful today as when they were first written. The author's key story in this sequence, 'The Call of Cthulhu', contains all the elements that set Lovecraft's half-glimpsed horrors apart from most other contributors to the pulps. Despite recent, misguided attempts to re-define the author's standing in the genre by people who have probably never read him, Lovecraft remains possibly the most influential author in horror after Edgar Allan Poe. I included this story and all the author's other macabre fiction in the definitive two-volume set Jo Fletcher and I put together for Gollancz some years ago, once again illustrated by the incomparable Les Edwards. The first volume, *Necronomicon: The Best Weird Tales of H.P. Lovecraft*, has now sold more copies than any other book I've ever been involved with.

Yours Truly, Jack the Ripper by Robert Bloch. Best known as the author of the original novel Alfred Hitchcock based his 1960 movie *Psycho* on, Robert Bloch (1917–94) was equally at home writing supernatural and psychological horror fiction. In his later years he became a much-respected film and TV scriptwriter in Hollywood, but his stories also appeared in a wide variety of magazines and anthologies. 'Yours Truly, Jack the Ripper' skillfully combines both of the author's fictional styles while casting the historical serial killer as an immortal being. Bloch's story was adapted by Barré Lyndon for a memorable episode of the TV series *Thriller*, hosted by Boris Karloff, and the author returned to the "Ripper" theme a number of times—not least for his own *Star Trek* script, 'Wolf in the Fold'. I included 'Yours Truly, Jack the Ripper' in my Robinson anthology *Psycho-Mania!*, which also featured a previously unpublished Introduction by Robert Bloch.

MY TOP TEN HORROR STORIES

STICKS by KARL EDWARD WAGNER. Although not a contemporary disciple of Lovecraft's like Robert Bloch was, big, bearded Southerner Karl Edward Wagner (1945–94) was one of the finest modern writers of horror fiction (as well as heroic fantasy), who died at a ridiculously young age. Also an esteemed critic and editor (with his own *Year's Best Horror* anthology series for DAW Books), Wagner's British Fantasy Award-winning 'Sticks' was a chilling tribute not only to *Weird Tales* illustrator Lee Brown Coye, but also to the type of cosmic horror that Lovecraft popularized in his own fiction. The story was also one of several acknowledged influences on the acclaimed HBO mini-series *True Detective*. I collected all Karl's darker stories and novellas in the two-volume *The Best Horror Stories of Karl Edward Wagner* for Centipede Press some years ago and, more recently, 'Sticks' is also included in my anthology *The Mammoth Book of Folk Horror*.

THE CHIMNEY by RAMSEY CAMPBELL. Ramsey Campbell (b. 1946) started his career as a teenager, writing pastiches of Lovecraft, but he soon developed his own style of urban horror based around his home city of Liverpool, England. Aptly described by the *Oxford Companion to English Literature* as "Britain's most respected living horror writer", Campbell has produced a prolific number of novels and short stories, with most of his work falling into the category of "best in genre". Choosing a favorite would difficult—there are just so many—so I will go for the World Fantasy Award-winning 'The Chimney', one of the creepiest Christmas horror stories I've ever read, given an extra poignant twist by the author's own—often disturbing—childhood experiences. I haven't yet done a Christmas reprint anthology but, if I did, 'The Chimney' would definitely be in it!

ONE FOR THE ROAD by STEPHEN KING. No list of favorite horror stories would be complete without something by Stephen King (b. 1947), who has been the most successful horror writer of the past five decades. As much as I love so many of his short stories, I would probably go for his tale 'One for the Road', a coda-of-sorts to the author's mega-vampire novel *'Salem's Lot*. King's writing style has always been deceptively simple, which allows the horror in his stories to come through loud and clear. Here it is given an extra poignancy by the fate of the family the two old-timers set out to rescue during a blizzard. PS Publishing issued a beautifully illustrated limited hardcover edition of this story a few years ago.

THE DARK COUNTRY by DENNIS ETCHISON. In my opinion, one of the greatest American short-story writers—in *any* genre—was Californian Dennis Etchison (1943–2019). Though a lot less prolific than some of his contemporaries, like King he began publishing in the late 1960s/early '70s, producing some remarkably lean and disturbing short stories, along with novels and screenplays. Having accompanied him South of the Border on a number of occasions, I would select Etchison's World Fantasy Award-winning 'The Dark Country'—not a horror story *per se*, but one of the best "stranger in strange lands" stories I have ever read. I only wish he had written more. I first published this story in *Fantasy Tales*, the small press magazine I co-edited with David A. Sutton, and I've since selected it in my "holiday horror" anthology *Summer Chills* and *The Mammoth Book of Folk Stories*.

DANCE OF THE DEAD by RICHARD MATHESON. Although widely regarded as a science fiction writer, Richard Matheson (1926–2013) was published in most genres during his lifetime. I have no hesitation in claiming him as a horror author—if only for his novels *I Am Legend* and *Hell House*, or his quartet of *Shock!* collections. Like his friend and contemporary Robert Bloch, Matheson also had the ability to add a psychological twist to his darker tales. I guess its futuristic setting makes 'Dance of the Dead' science fiction, but with its experimental style and grim subject matter, it wouldn't be out of place in any horror anthology. In fact, I included it in *Don't Turn Out the Light*, the third of the new "Not at Night" anthologies that I edited for PS Publishing.

THE MAN WHO DREW CATS by MICHAEL MARSHALL SMITH. A natural successor to both King and Matheson, in part thanks to his lean writing style, is British author Michael Marshall Smith (b. 1965), who has gone on to publish a number of successful crime/thriller novels under the not-so-subtle pseudonym "Michael

Marshall". He won the British Fantasy Award for his first short story, 'The Man Who Drew Cats', which I had the pleasure of originally publishing when David Sutton and I co-edited *Dark Voices: The Pan Book of Horror*. I used it again in the second volume of *Best New Horror*, *The Best of Best New Horror Volume One*, and my children's anthology *Terrifying Tales to Tell at Night: 10 Scary Stories to Give You Nightmares!*. Shamelessly inspired by the author's love of Stephen King's work, with its effortless narrative and nasty twist ending, the story could easily have come from the imagination of that writer. As it happens, it turned out to be pure Michael Marshall Smith, and he has gone on to become one of the most accomplished short story writers of his generation.

Homecoming / The October People / Uncle Einar by Ray Bradbury. Like his friend Richard Matheson, most people probably think of Ray Bradbury (1920–2012) as a science fiction writer, and they would not be wrong in that assessment. But while, as a young man, Bradbury was cutting his teeth in the SF pulp magazines, he was also contributing an equal number of tales to such periodicals as *Weird Tales*. To read Bradbury is to read imaginative prose at its very best. His fiction can transport you to other worlds or far futures, or just as easily bring you back to Earth with a shudder and a bump (in the night). I would recommend his novel *Something Wicked This Way Comes* to any young reader as an introduction to the horror genre, and I adore his stories about the Eternal Family—a sort of literary precursor to The Addams Family and The Munsters. Collected together in *From the Dust Returned*, these stories are in turns lyrical, poignant and chilling. This final entry is a bit of a cheat, as I would happily choose 'Homecoming' or 'The October People' or 'Uncle Einar'—take your pick: they are all as wonderfully macabre as each other.

So there you have it, ten or so of the very best in my opinion, and taken together a wonderful introduction to some of the finest short fiction that the horror genre has to offer. And if some enterprising publisher wanted to offer me the opportunity to put them all together in a volume entitled *10 Top Tales of Terror*, or something similar, then you know where to find me . . .

STEPHEN JONES

Stephen Jones lives in London, England. A Hugo Award nominee, he is the winner of four World Fantasy Awards, three International Horror Guild Awards, five Bram Stoker Awards, twenty-one British Fantasy Awards, and a Lifetime Achievement Award from the Horror Writers Association. One of Britain's most acclaimed horror and dark fantasy writers and editors, he has more than 155 books to his credit, including the acclaimed illustrated histories *The Art of Horror*, *The Art of Horror Movies*, and *The Art of Pulp Horror*, the film books of Neil Gaiman's *Coraline* and *Stardust*, *The Illustrated Monster Movie Guide*, *The Hellraiser Chronicles*, and the non-fiction studies *Horror: 100 Best Books* and *Horror: Another 100 Best Books* (both with Kim Newman), along with such anthologies as *The Lovecraft Squad* and *Zombie Apocalypse!* series and thirty volumes of *Best New Horror*. A Guest of Honor at the 2002 World Fantasy Convention in Minneapolis, Minnesota, and the 2004 World Horror Convention in Phoenix, Arizona, he has been a guest lecturer at UCLA in California and London's Kingston University and St. Mary's University College. You can visit his web site at *www.stephenjoneseditor.com* or follow him on Facebook at "Stephen Jones-Editor".

Website: **www.stephenjoneseditor.com**

EXQUISITE CORPSE

Author: **Poppy Z. Brite**
Publisher: Gallery Books
Year of Publication: 1996
Genre: Horror
Typology: Novel
Total Score: 93
Goodreads Score: 3,75

Escaped from Painswick prison, serial killer Andrew Compton searches for a place to live where he will be able to satisfy his ever-unquenched thirst for blood. The journey takes him to New Orleans and into the arms of Jay Byrne, a dark charmed photographer who awakens Compton's murderous instincts. But the man turns out to be anything but a sacrificial victim. It is this encounter between two dark souls which soon ends up involving Tran, a Vietnamese boy rejected by his family because of his homosexuality, who is on the run from a psychotic lover. Against the backdrop of the decadent French Quarter and lashed by the invectives of the illegal WHIV radio begins a macabre dance of love and death, necrophilia, cannibalism and loneliness. A spiritual autopsy which plunges the scalpel into living flesh to feed us a darker side of the soul. A cult book of the genre (though not for everyone, given its strong and explicit content), this beautifully written tale was partly inspired by Jeffrey Dahmer, the well-known Milwaukee cannibal.

FEARFUL SYMMETRIES

Author: **Thomas F. Monteleone**
Publisher: Cemetery Dance
Year of Publication: 2004
Genre: Horror / Thriller
Typology: Story Collection
Total Score: 84
Goodreads Score: 4.10

An eclectic assembly of 27 short stories, this collection retraces more than 20 years of the author's career through a variety of themes and styles, with forays into different genres and subgenres including supernatural horror, psychological thrillers and suspense. Monteleone's writing is of a high standard, deftly shifting across the dark, funny, brutal, ironic, and the disturbing. The mood and characters of each story are crafted with insight and staged through an original writing style. Here some classic horror tropes are taken up and reinterpreted, such as vampires or Lovecraftian monsters. Among my favorite stories are *Rehearsals*, *The Night is Freezing Fast*, *Prodigal Son* and *Triptych di Amore*.

FEVER DREAM

Author: **Samanta Schweblin**
Publisher: Riverhead
Year of Publication: 2014
Genre: Horror / Thriller
Typology: Novel
Total Score: 86
Goodreads Score: 3,74

The first work by this Argentinian author to be translated into English, this ghost story explores the relationship between parent and child, the transmigration of the soul, and current events and their consequences (like the use of pesticides in Argentina). What makes Schweblin's voice compelling is her precise prose and how she uses it to probe the most complex dynamics of the human soul. This novel begins as a narration by the fevered Amanda as she lies on a bed waiting to die, with a child, David, beside her. The surreal dialogue (and contrasts) between the two characters reveals the events which took place a few days earlier, in which the precocious David was the original protagonist. Their narratives guide the reader, untangling the complex underpinnings of the tale into its core until reaching its disturbing center.

FIEND

Author: **Peter Stenson**
Publisher: Crown
Year of Publication: 2013
Genre: Horror
Typology: Novel
Total Score: 83
Goodreads Score: 3,55

With *Fiend* we come back to the zombie subgenre— handled once again in an original way, and accompanied by other symbolic interpretations. This story makes use of methamphetamine (a disturbing 'chemical' demon) as a vehicle, utilizing meth-induced hallucinations and the realities of addiction to drive the narrative. The protagonist, Chase Daniels, is a perfect anti-hero. Besides having to deal with an existence destroyed by drugs (for which he has sold everything, including love and family), he finds himself facing the end of the world... complete with zombies. But perhaps, despite everything, a new possibility (or hope) has opened up for Chase? The author manages to juggle the thoughts, memories and hallucinations of a junkie, describing each with incisiveness and inventiveness, and without forgetting to frame it all into an action horror novel about the undead. The author's prose is often minimalist, but no less effective.

FLEDGLING

Author: **Octavia E. Butler**
Publisher: Grand Central
Year of Publication: 2005
Genre: Horror / Thriller / Dark Fantasy
Typology: Novel
Total Score: 83
Goodreads Score: 3,86

An acclaimed African American science fiction author, in this novel Butler melds horror, thriller and dark fantasy works into the vampire subgenre, and details the results with complex metaphors, analogies and reflections on class, race and sex. The novel tells the story of the young (and black) Shori who, suffering from amnesia and unable to explain her unusual needs and abilities, discovers she is a genetically modified vampire. Hers is a breed shrouded in mystery: a hybridization with the need for symbiosis with human beings. This theme is masterfully combined with those of adolescence, the discovery of self, and other forms of personal transformation. With this work, the author breaks free from worn genre patterns by proposing an interesting 'social fantasy'.

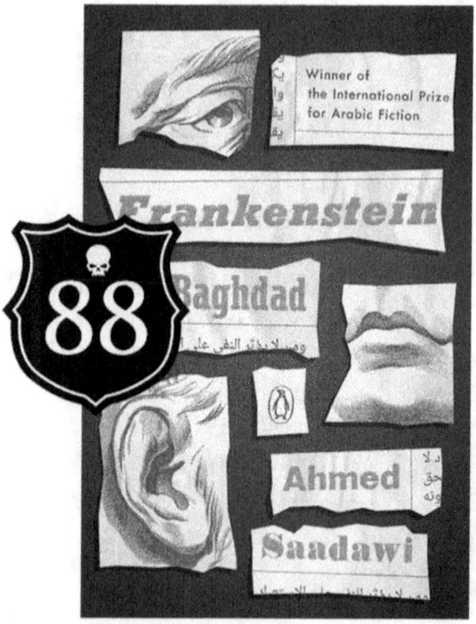

FRANKENSTEIN IN BAGHDAD

Author: **Ahmed Saadawi**
Publisher: Penguin Books
Year of Publication: 2013
Genre: Horror / Magic Realism
Typology: Novel
Total Score: 88
Goodreads Score: 3,55

A fascinating work introducing a surreal vision of contemporary Iraq. Saadawi offers us a retelling of the famous novel by Mary Shelley, this time set in the chaos of Iraq under US occupation. This is a dark work (but one also veiled with irony) animated by many fascinating characters, each of whom represents the diverse voices of that land. This time the monster is created by a junk dealer named Havi, who uses pieces of his friend Nahed's body. Nahed is the victim of a suicide bomb attack (metaphorically indicating the reconstruction of a dissolved civilization) and Havi's purpose is to give his friend a burial. To do this he needs a whole body, and he completes the missing parts with the remains of other victims. Saadawi's Frankenstein soon becomes a destroyer and a murderer, personifying the chaos and violence that reigns in Baghdad. It is difficult to judge the original author's style—since this is a translation from Arabic—but in English the tone and execution are highly enjoyable. This book, for the many complexities contained within, deserves to be read.

BEST 10 HORROR BOOKS FROM 1986 TO 2020
SELECTED BY

BRIAN EVENSON

DAWN by OCTAVIA E. BUTLER (1987)
GRIMSCRIBE: HIS LIVES AND WORKS by THOMAS LIGOTTI (1991)
COME CLOSER by SARA GRAN (2003)
20TH CENTURY GHOSTS by JOE HILL (2005)
A DARK MATTER by PETER STRAUB (2010)
THE BEAUTIFUL THING THAT AWAITS US ALL by LAIRD BARRON (2013)
FEVER DREAM by SAMANTA SCHWEBLIN (2014)
A HEAD FULL OF GHOSTS by PAUL TREMBLAY (2015)
THE FISHERMAN by JOHN LANGAN (2016)
THE ONLY GOOD INDIANS by STEPHEN GRAHAM JONES (2020)

BRIAN EVENSON is an award-winning American writer whose talent has lent itself across multiple genres. Among his works include *Father of Lies* (1998); *The Open Curtain* (2006); *Immobility* (2012); *A Collapse of Horses: Stories* (2016) and *Song for the Unraveling of the World* (2019). Website: www.brianevenson.com

GENERATION LOSS

Author: **Elizabeth Hand**
Publisher: Small Beer Press
Year of Publication: 2007
Genre: Horror / Thriller / Mystery
Typology: Novel
Total Score: 84
Goodreads Score: 3,78

A novel by a very talented author. In this thriller with fantastic elements (poised between the supernatural and a view into the effects of a sick mind), Hand introduces us to Cass Neary, a photographer who once had a good reputation during the punk scene of the '70s. Now aged and disgraced, she takes the opportunity to interview Aphrodite Kamestos, a colleague from the counterculture who originally inspired her. Their meeting will reveal a world of strangeness and horror. Beyond the beautiful prose and well-drawn settings, the connections with art and photography and its exploration of the fine line between genius and madness, this work crafts a fascinating view onto the dark beauty of the grotesque.

GHOST SUMMER

Author: **Tananarive Due**
Publisher: Prime Books
Year of Publication: 2015
Genre: Horror / Horror SciFi
Typology: Story Collection
Total Score: 91
Goodreads Score: 4,23

A collection of 14 short stories (and the titular novella) by a great writer, covering themes and subgenres such as racism (naturally very close to the author), pandemics, zombies, cloning, ghosts, shapeshifters, sexual predators and much more. Three of these stories form a sort of apocalyptic trilogy, while another three (with a supernatural flavour) link to the same setting of Francetown, a rural town in Georgia. Among my favorites tales are *Ghost Summer* (the novella), *The Lake, Patient Zero* and *Removal Order*. This book best summarizes all the characteristics and potential of 'speculative' fiction, and skilfully adds in horror and science fiction genres. The author's prose is brilliant, displaying her talent for evoking emotions via the shades of humanity offered by her lively characters.

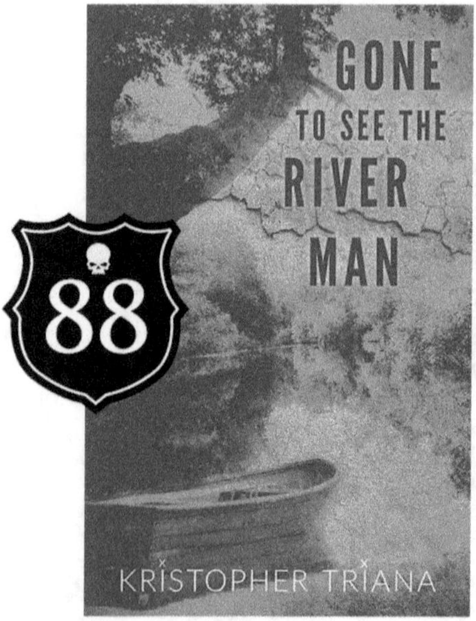

GONE TO SEE THE RIVER MAN

Author: **Kristopher Triana**
Publisher: Cemetery Dance
Year of Publication: 2020
Genre: Horror / Extreme Horror
Typology: Novel
Total Score: 88
Goodreads Score: 4,27

An author who might fit better in the ranks of Extreme Horror than in Splatterpunk, Triana shows a versatility and ability to move across multiple genres in his works. This short novel is less gory than his previous offerings, animating the controversial character of Lori: a woman obsessed with serial killers. Drawn to Edmund Cox, a sadist who has massacred more than 20 women, Lori tries to get close to him—first by writing him letters and then visiting him in prison. The story takes shape when Cox entrusts her with a task: she must meet the so-called 'River Man' along the banks of the winding river Hollow, where many murder victims have been mutilated and dismembered. With its smooth rhythm and well-formed characters, this book blends suspense, cosmic horror and strong content with a brutal ending.

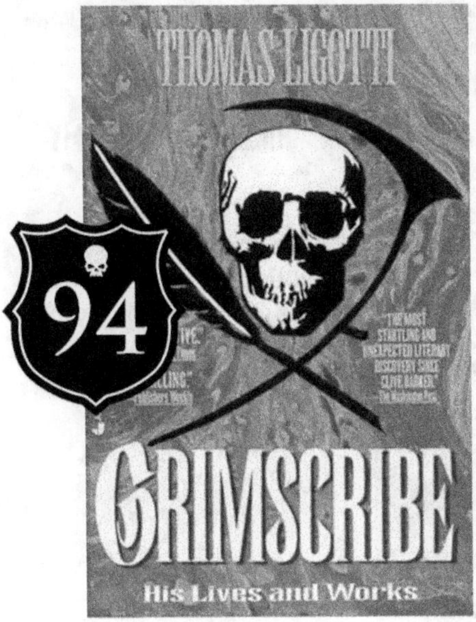

GRIMSCRIBE
HIS LIVES AND WORKS

Author: **Thomas Ligotti**
Publisher: Jove
Year of Publication: 1991
Genre: Horror / Weird / Modern Gothic
Typology: Story Collection
Total Score : 94
Goodreads Score: 4,15

The second collection of 12 short stories (and better than the first such offering, *Songs of a Dead Dreamer*) by an author considered a cult master of the genre. In these stories Ligotti pays homage, in unique style, to some of the greats such as Lovecraft, Poe, Blackwood and Hawthorne. From cosmic and psychological horror the author branches off into other directions, extending the visions from which he draws inspiration and bringing us closer to existential discomfort and concern over our more arcane natures. My favorite stories include *Nethescurial*, *In the Shadow of Another World*, *The Last Feast of Harlequin* and *The Night School*. The deep, disturbing and philosophical prose opens imaginary windows onto the psyche. A brilliant author, but not for everyone.

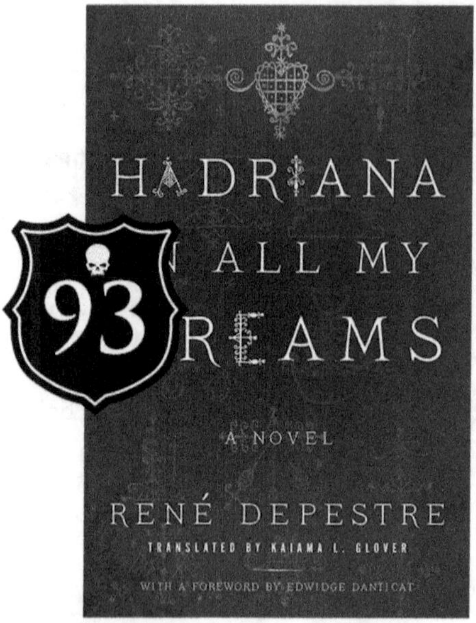

HADRIANA IN ALL MY DREAMS

Author: **René Depestre**
Publisher: Akashic Books
Year of Publication: 1988
Genre: Horror / Magic Realism
Typology: Novel
Total Score: 93
Goodreads Score: 3,56

René Depestre is a Haitian writer and poet. One of the most important voices of his country, he lived for many years in exile in France and Cuba. Set in the late 1930s in the Haitian village of Jacmel, in this novel a young French woman, Hadriana, is preparing to get married—but the morning before the wedding, she drinks a mysterious potion and transforms into a zombie. She is buried and then brought back to life by a sorcerer, becoming a popular legend. The story deals with the themes of race, sexuality and the right to happiness (even of the dead), enchanting the reader with voodoo culture and Haitian folklore. Written in refined, satirical, sensual and lush first-person prose and poising it between horror and magic realism, this book is for readers with fine tastes.

HAIR SIDE, FLESH SIDE

Author: **Helen Marshall**
Publisher: ChiZine
Year of Publication: 2012
Genre: Horror / Weird
Typology: Story Collection
Total Score: 90
Goodreads Score: 3,90

The debut short story collection by Canadian author Helen Marshall, a genre interpreter to watch. This mix of 15 tales is spiced with a weird and fantastic sauce and warped by the surreal, showing a vivid, lyrical prose well-combined with the mood and soul of the stories. Particularly original is the short story *Sandition*, which tells of an unfinished Jane Austin novel written inside a woman. This is a work which fans of books (and of libraries and manuscripts) will surely appreciate. Among my other favorite stories are *No Ghosts in London*, *Dead White Men*, and *In the High Places of the World*. A sophisticated, elegant and disturbing collection.

BEST 10 HORROR ANTHOLOGIES FROM 1986 TO 2020
SELECTED BY

ERIC J. GUIGNARD

PRIME EVIL Edited by DOUGLAS E. WINTER (1988)
THE BEST OF SHADOWS Edited by CHARLES L. GRANT (1988)
RAZORED SADDLES Edited by JOE R. LANSDALE and PAUL LOBRUTTO (1989)
BORDERLANDS 2 Edited by THOMAS F. MONTELEONE (1991)
THE BEST OF WHISPERS Edited by STUART DAVID SCHIFF (1994)
THE MAMMOTH BOOK OF BEST NEW HORROR – VOLUME TEN
Edited by STEPHEN JONES (2013)
WASTERLANDS: STORIES OF THE APOCALYPSE
Edited by JOHN JOSEPH ADAMS (2008)
DEMONS: ENCOUNTERS WITH THE DEVIL AND HIS MINIONS,
FALLEN ANGELS, AND THE POSSESSED Edited by JOHN SKIPP (2011)
THE YEAR'S BEST DARK FANTASY AND HORROR 2014
Edited by PAULA GURAN (2014)
THE BEST OF THE BEST HORROR OF THE YEAR: 10 YEARS OF ESSENTIAL
SHORT HORROR FICTION Edited by ELLEN DATLOW (2018)

ERIC J. GUIGNARD is an award-winning American writer and editor.
Some of the anthologies he has edited include *Dark Tales of Lost Civilizations* (2012), *After Death* (2013), *A World of Horror* (2018) and *Pop the Clutch: Thrilling Tales of Rockabilly, Monsters, and Hot Rod Horror* (2019).
Website: www.ericguignard.com

HAUNTED

Author: **Chuck Palahniuk**
Publisher: Anchor
Year of Publication: 2005
Genre: Horror / Bizzarro
Typology: Novel / Story Collection
Total Score: 94
Goodreads Score: 3,60

A collection of 23 interconnected stories, each of which gives voice to a different character, forming an atypical novel. The author is brilliant, as demonstrated by his other books which likewise escape a precise genre 'label'. But too much rigidity in categorization risks confusing rather than clarifying things for the reader, especially here. The anthology-style story begins with a group of writers locked up in an abandoned cinema. In this setting, each will try to write their masterpiece with the hope of achieving success once they are released. Their individual experiences emerge in the stories (and poems) that make up this work. The amusing, revolting, mind-blowing, extreme and explicit content qualifies this book as an entry in this guide as a horror/thriller mixed with bizarro fiction. Using minimalist prose in the form of flashbacks, Palahniuk's writing is always recognizable, powerful and unique.

HEADER 2

Author: **Edward Lee**
Publisher: Camelot
Year of Publication: 2010
Genre: Hardcore Horror / Extreme Horror
Typology: Novel
Total Score: 90
Goodreads Score: 4.07

Edward Lee is the commander of hardcore/extreme horror. This novel is the sequel to his novella 'Header', and treats us to Lee at the top of his crazy form. The story details the bloody (and historic) feud between the 'men of the hills' (the notorious American rednecks frequently portrayed by the author in his various works) led by old Helton Tuckton and his family, and the ferocious mafia gang headed by Paul III Vinchetti. A spiral of wickedness on both sides (including the infamous 'header', which stands out as the most effective way to repay a wrong suffered) unwinds, destined to culminate precisely on Christmas day. These pages offer disturbing and grotesque descriptions, with highly explicit content. Often revolting (but not lacking in irony), the novel offers a vivid picture of rural America as rarely found in other books regardless of genre. A book only for fans of the extreme.

HER BODY AND OTHER PARTIES

Author: **Carmen Maria Machado**
Publisher: Graywolf Press
Year of Publication: 2017
Genre: Horror / Dark Fantasy / SciFi
Typology: Story Collection
Total Score: 93
Goodreads Score: 3,92

A remarkable debut collection of eight stories ranging from psychological horror, the bizarre, fantasy and science fiction, these stories share the female world in an original, visceral and surprising way which aims straight at the experience of one's own body. Between sexual assaults, self-inflicted violence, ancient traumas, the exploration of desire, young mothers and phantasmagoric police procedures, the female perspective here is not only highly original but also unconventional and courageous in its portrayal. This is a provocative and innovative work with a strong vision. Among my favorite stories include *Difficult at Parties*, *The Husband Stitch*, *Real Women Have Bodies*, *Eight Bites*.

HOUSE OF LEAVES

Author: **Mark Z. Danielewski**
Publisher: Random House
Year of Publication: 2000
Genre: Horror / Magic Realism
Typology: Novel
Total Score: 95
Goodreads Score: 4,05

A very peculiar work which might best be defined as experimental literary horror, combining magic realism, poetry and many other elements. The story follows Pulitzer Prize-winner Will Navidson and his family as they move into a new house, where some odd spatial characteristics and variable dimensions betray that their new home may not be subject to the laws of physics. This surreal house-labyrinth is the true main character of the novel, and the exploration of it (detailed via video materials known as The Navidson Records) guides the reader through the book. This one is not an easy read due to its layout and structure, characterized by peculiar text arrangements. Experimentalism is evident in all aspects of this literary work, making it a metaphor for the labyrinthine house it details. A fascinating novel, this will not be enjoyed by everyone due to the extreme complexity of its design and vision.

HOUSES WITHOUT DOORS

Author: **Peter Straub**
Publisher: Random House
Year of Publication: 1990
Genre: Horror / Psychological Horror
Typology: Novel
Total Score : 87
Goodreads Score: 3,75

A collection of 13 short stories by a master of the genre known for his literary interpretations of the dark world. The author's common subjects (murderers, child molesters, haunted houses) take a backseat in this book, where the charm lies instead in the author's ability to uncover the wonders of even the most common aspects of life. Straub guides us through his explorations into emotions, from hate to jealousy, from fear to guilt, where the reader is fully immersed. Among my favorite stories are *The Juniper Tree*, *The Buffalo Hunter*, *Mrs God* and *Blue Rose*. Straub is not an easy author for a typical genre fans to appreciate; his postmodern style is different from many other writers. For this reason, I think a collection of his stories may be the best way to first approach his work.

IN SILENT GRAVES

Author: **Gary A. Braunbeck**
Publisher: Leisure
Year of Publication: 2004
Genre: Horror / Dark Fantasy
Typology: Novel
Total Score: 86
Goodreads Score: 3,79

The world of journalist Robert Londrigan, which seems perfect, is turned abruptly upside down when he encounters a mysterious, horrific figure in the park–beginning our journey into the protagonist's grotesque and heartbreaking nightmare. The revelations that follow will be many, including an alternate reality which unmasks all horrors. As always, the prose is of high quality for this great interpreter (recommended for more discerning readers), and the story's sparse action scenes allow space to better highlight the subtler characteristics of this work.

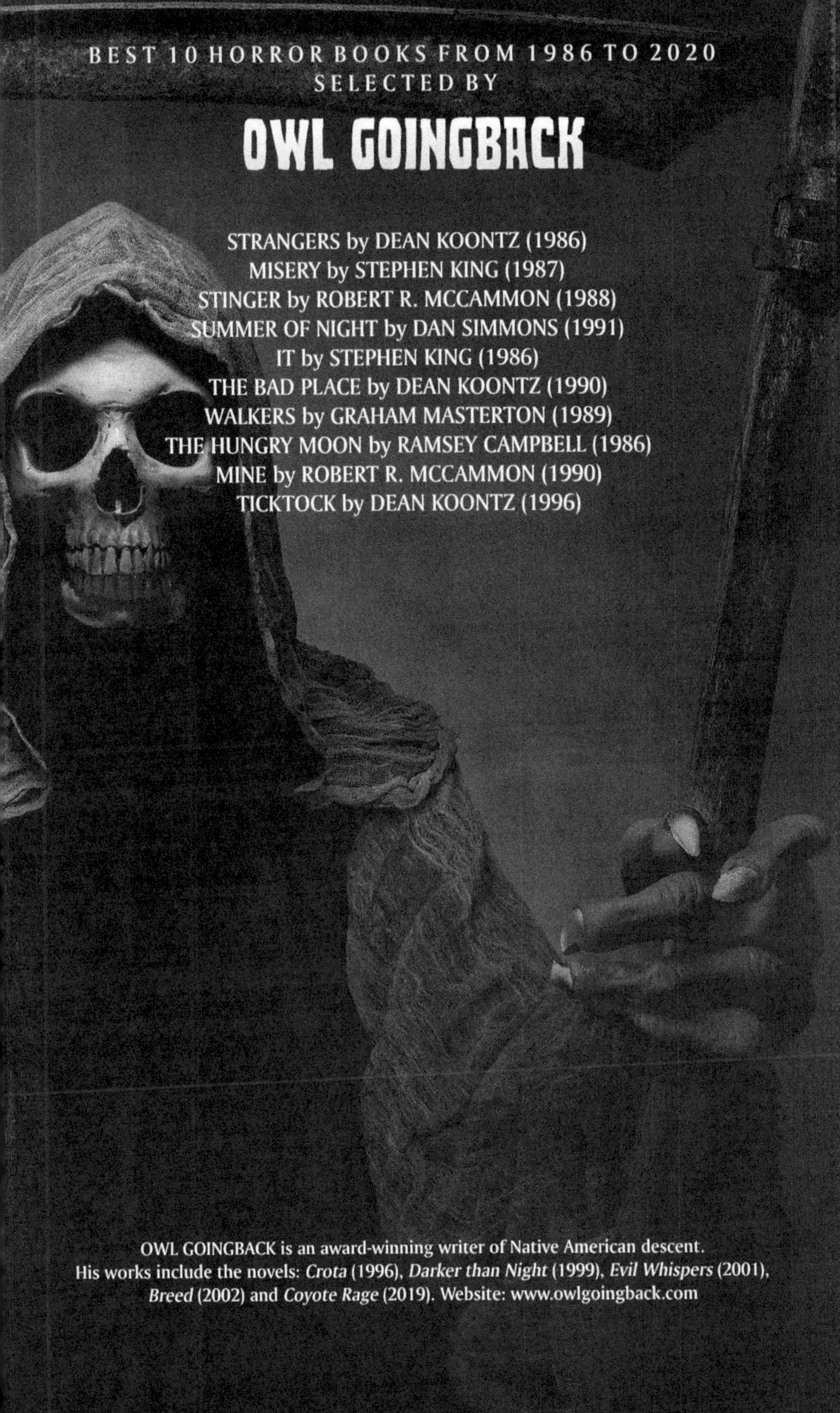

BEST 10 HORROR BOOKS FROM 1986 TO 2020
SELECTED BY

OWL GOINGBACK

STRANGERS by DEAN KOONTZ (1986)
MISERY by STEPHEN KING (1987)
STINGER by ROBERT R. MCCAMMON (1988)
SUMMER OF NIGHT by DAN SIMMONS (1991)
IT by STEPHEN KING (1986)
THE BAD PLACE by DEAN KOONTZ (1990)
WALKERS by GRAHAM MASTERTON (1989)
THE HUNGRY MOON by RAMSEY CAMPBELL (1986)
MINE by ROBERT R. MCCAMMON (1990)
TICKTOCK by DEAN KOONTZ (1996)

OWL GOINGBACK is an award-winning writer of Native American descent. His works include the novels: *Crota* (1996), *Darker than Night* (1999), *Evil Whispers* (2001), *Breed* (2002) and *Coyote Rage* (2019). Website: www.owlgoingback.com

INK

Author: **Jonathan Maberry**
Publisher: St. Martin's Griffin
Year of Publication: 2020
Genre: Horror / Thriller
Typology: Novel
Total Score: 85
Goodreads Score: 4,03

The idea of a memory thief is certainly captivating, and Maberry develops it very well in this intense supernatural thriller. Private Detective Monk Addison—whose skin is covered with the tattooed faces of murder victims—moves to Pine Deep, where his tattooist friend Patty Cakes lives. When the tattoos on other locals begin to fade, their associated memories also disappear—becoming part of a strange new predator's experience. This novel, which completely reinterprets the theme of vampirism, is engaging and well-crafted, with strong characters. Suggested for all readers.

ISLAND

Author: **Richard Laymon**
Publisher: Leisure
Year of Publication: 1991
Genre: Horror / Thriller / Slasher
Typology: Novel
Total Score: 85
Goodreads Score: 3,80

A high-voltage thriller/slasher novel, written in an engaging diary style. The imprint of an author like Laymon is evident here in his narrative rhythm, the strong and spicy content, and his vivid characters. 18-year-old Rupert Conway joins his girlfriend Connie's family on a boat trip across the Caribbean. But the vacation is short-lived once their yacht mysteriously explodes, stranding everyone on a desert island. But the island is not as uninhabited as it seems—someone hides in the thick jungle, targeting the castaways one at a time... and this intelligent and perverse predator seems to have very specific objectives. The novel follows a raving manhunt, and is full of surprises, wickedness and depravity. The finish is creative and unpredictable.

IT

Author: **Stephen King**
Publisher: New English Library
Year of Publication: 1986
Genre: Horror
Typology: Novel
Total Score: 92
Goodreads Score: 4,24

This is one of King's most famous and best-appreciated novels, so there's no need to summarize the plot or to describe the events which await the reader. The success of this coming-of-age novel is largely due to the (primordial and highly symbolic) character of Pennywise, who embodies the fears of the unknown and the uncertainties which torment adolescence. The Losers Club, to which the group of young protagonists belongs, represents a mirror of friendship and loyalty which remains even into adulthood. We all have different fears, and the choice of the shape-shifting 'monster' is really effective. Perhaps verbose in some parts (though well-written, and from the time of extra-long novels), the story is embellished with a writing style that knows how to capture the essence and memory of youth. This is a cult favorite of the genre which every fan must have and keep.

JOHN DIES AT THE END

Author: **David Wong**
Publisher: Permuted Press
Year of Publication: 2007
Genre: Horror / Bizzarro Fiction
Typology: Novel
Total Score: 82
Goodreads Score: 3,89

An entertaining tale, told in a frenzied rhythm, which follows the story of paranormal investigators John and Dave as they take on demonic and monstrous entities. Thanks to a strange substance called 'Soy Sauce' they are able to see supernatural and interdimensional beings. When a group of dark beings conspires against the world, it's up to this duo to deal with it. The book is stuffed with surreal creatures, and the author's tongue-in-cheek sense of irony never fails, even amid generous offerings of bloodshed (and more). Recommended for readers who are looking for a crazy and anarchic SciFi horror adventure mixed with urban fantasy elements, and who aren't shy of dirty jokes and disgusting interludes. A dark comedy like this—with its original, irreverent, surrealist take on pop culture—always finds fans. Humor doesn't stand in opposition to intelligence. In fact, as this books demonstrates, it's often quite the opposite.

KIN

Author: **Kealan Patrick Burke**
Publisher: Cemetery Dance
Year of Publication: 2011
Genre: Horror / Slasher
Typology: Novel
Total Score: 87
Goodreads Score: 3,94

This novel has a slasher soul in the tradition of Laymon or Ketchum. It's a summer day in Elkwood, Alabama, and Claire Lambert—a survivor of real atrocities—staggers a country road, naked and injured, where she is saved at the last moment. The novel opens with this impactful scene—but it's a mere snapshot of the Elkwood massacre, of which Claire is the only survivor. Far from the end of a story, this opening is just the beginning. Revenge, and the ways people are transformed by their experiences, guides the story that follows, showing how the line can be blurred between good and evil, predator and prey. Also masterfully handled is the theme of family relationships, and how these are affected by traumatic events. Burke's style holds nothing back, an approach which fits well with the feel of this work. Each character's soul and psychology is well-defined and crafted by this talented author.

LADY BITS

Author: **Kate Jonez**
Publisher: Journalstone
Year of Publication: 2019
Genre: Horror
Typology: Story Collection
Total Score: 83
Goodreads Score: 3,98

This is a compelling collection of 16 short stories by a fascinating interpreter of the genre. The themes Jonez develops in her tales touch various aspects of the female psyche. The women protagonists of these stories are authentic without being obscured by clichés, and each comes complete with complex, sometimes unpredictable, positive and negative characters—as is human nature. The genre blends the supernatural with the mysterious, featuring creatures, magic and folklore, all intertwined with a new gothic atmosphere. This is a rich book to explore. Among my favorite stories are *Carnivores*, *Envy*, *Mountain*, *A Flicker of Light on Devil's Night* and *All the Day You'll Have Good Luck*.

BEST 10 HORROR BOOKS
SELECTED BY

JOHN SKIPP

THE OCTOBER COUNTRY by RAY BRADBURY (1955)
STORIES THEY WOULDN'T LET ME DO ON TV
Edited by ALFRED HITCHCOCK (1957)
DEATHBIRD STORIES by HARLAN ELLISON (1975)
THE SHEEP LOOK UP by JOHN BRUNNER (1972)
GRENDEL by JOHN GARDER (1971)
TALES OF MYSTERY AND IMAGINATION by EDGAR ALLAN POE (1842)
LORD OF THE FLIES by WILLIAM GOLDING (1954)
THE CIPHER by KATHE KOJA (1991)
RADIANT DOWN / RAVENOUS DUSK by CODY GOODFELLOW (2000/2003)
APESHIT by CARLTON MELLICK III (2008)

JOHN SKIPP is an American writer and editor, and is one of the original creators of the Splatterpunk movement. Some of his novels include *The Light at the End* (1986, written with Craig Spector), *The Bridge* (1991, written with Craig Spector), *Animals* (1992, written with Craig Spector), *The Long Last Call* (2006), *The Day Before* (2006, written with Cody Goodfellow), *Spore* (2010, written with Cody Goodfellow) and *The Art of Horrible People* (2015).

LET THE RIGHT ONE IN

Author: **John A. Lindqvist**
Publisher: Quercus
Year of Publication: 2004
Genre: Horror / Thriller
Typology: Novel
Total Score: 82
Goodreads Score: 4,03

1981. In Blackeberg, a seedy suburb of Stockholm (where the author was born), the body of a teenager is found drained of blood. Ritual murder is suspected. Oskar, the protagonist, is a 12-year-old boy bullied by his classmates and suffering difficult relations with his parents. His befriends Eli, a girl of his age who has moved to the neighbourhood—but Eli turns out to be a vampire, and here the story moves forward. The author's prose, while not overly detailed, effectively conveys the characters and tones of the tale. A novel on the vampire trope, the themes here quickly turn into metaphors for marginalization, adolescence and addiction (alcoholism), further exploring subjects such as pedophilia and loneliness as it describes a far-away country depicted with a blend of realism and disenchantment.

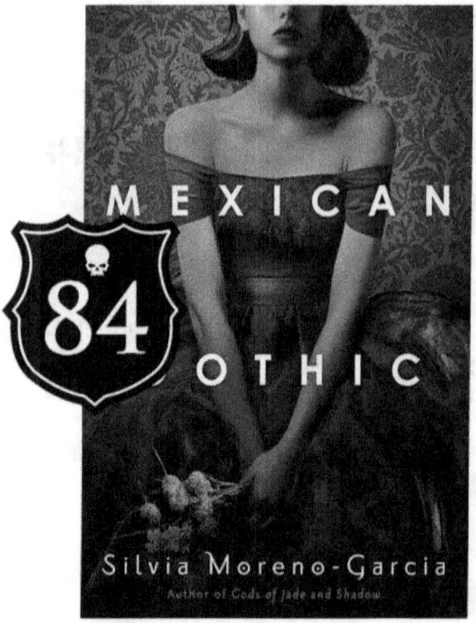

MEXICAN GOTHIC

Author: **Silvia Moreno Garcia**
Publisher: Del Rey
Year of Publication: 2020
Genre: Horror / Mystery
Typology: Novel
Total Score: 84
Goodreads Score: 3,70

1950s. 22-year-old Noemí Taboada, a determined and courageous woman, receives a disturbing letter from her cousin Catalina, asking for help with a mysterious problem. Without hesitation, our heroine heads to High Place, an old villa in the Mexican countryside. Situated near the former mining town of El Triunfo, the enigmatic home of the Doyle family hides many secrets. A whirlwind of horrifying events set off right away... but in this story, we are far from the usual haunted house clichés. The author, offering an original postcolonial interpretation of well-trod themes, uses a vivid, classically-styled prose (suitable for the era of the setting) that speaks to every type of reader. Among the themes in this book include racism and Mexican folklore.

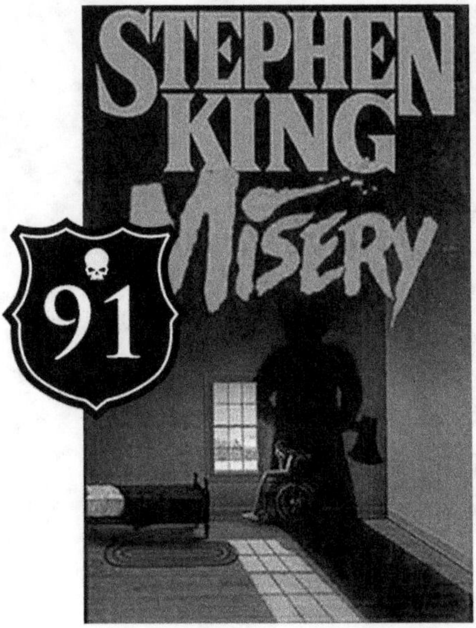

MISERY

Author: **Stephen King**
Publisher: New English
Year of Publication: 1987
Genre: Horror / Thriller
Typology: Novel
Total Score: 91
Goodreads Score: 4,18

Another famous King novel, this one is more a thriller than a horror story. Following a car accident in remote Colorado, bestselling writer Paul Sheldon is rescued by ex-nurse Annie Wilkes (one of his biggest fans) who takes him into her house to care for him while he recovers. In Sheldon's latest novel, *Misery's Son*, the popular protagonist dies in childbirth, and the demise of Wilkes' favourite heroine devastates the already unstable caregiver. This leads her to keep Sheldon prisoner, forcing him to write a new book that brings Misery Chastain back to life—a task he undertakes in a crescendo of brutality and torture (and barbiturates). This novel works well despite the presence of only two characters, and each of them is skilfully captured by the author from a psychological point of view. The male protagonist betrays autobiographical features of King himself.

MISTER SUICIDE

Author: **Nicole Cushing**
Publisher: Word Horde
Year of Publication: 2015
Genre: Horror
Typology: Novel
Total Score: 85
Goodreads Score: 3,71

This fascinating first novel by Cushing is written in the second person (an unusual and courageous choice), placing the reader inside the head of the protagonist along a dark and morbid journey. A portrait of the onset of madness, this story follows the degeneration of a young man through his disturbed and self-destructive impulses, describing the genesis of a psychopath. The main character is a misfit and troubled teenager with violent parents and no friends, who finds himself prey to bullying by his peers. And then there is Mister Suicide: a sick, independent consciousness, an ambiguous voice which speaks in his head, trying to convince him to take his own life. The discovery of an extreme pornography magazine (*Perfect Monsters*) and a place for perverse entertainment will lead the young man along a torrid initiation. Topics covered by the book include the abuse of minors and psychosis. Some of this content is very strong and disturbing; this one is not for everyone.

MY EARLY CRIMES

Author: **Paolo Di Orazio**
Publisher: Raven's Head Press
Year of Publication: 2015
Genre: Horror / Splatterpunk
Typology: Story Collection
Total Score: 87
Goodreads Score: 4,00

A collection by Italian writer Paolo Di Orazio, containing ten stories about children committing or witnessing their first murder. This book—originally published in Italian in 1989 (and which roused a surreal parliamentary question regarding art as incitement to commit murder) and attached to the horror comic *Splatter*—could be considered part of the early splatterpunk movement. Nine killers confess to their first murders in first person; they are not serial nor professional killers, but teenagers, children, boys who kill in self-defense or out of madness or revenge, or for fun, or as an act of desperation. Through these stories, the author guides us into the minds of children and adults and the relations between them within late '80s society. An innovative book with explicit content, this one is recommended only for the fans of the genre.

MOON ON THE WATER

Author: **Mort Castle**
Publisher: Leisure
Year of Publication: 2001
Genre: Horror
Typology: Story Collection
Total Score: 85
Goodreads Score: 3,71

Mort Castle is a very original author, and in short fiction he offers the best of his work in the genre: writing in a way that is irreverent, literary and highly personal. In my opinion this collection of short stories summarizes all the characteristics and peculiarities of his vision, approaching various literary and artistic references with subtle irony and in a way which continuously experiments (his influences range from Hemingway to Romero, and many more). The themes touched on in his works are heterogeneous: loss, personal demons, the weakness of the human condition. I could describe this collection as a sort of 'jazz' of horror. Among my favorite stories are *The Old Man and the Dead*, and *Henderson's Place/The Girl with the Summer Eyes*.

NIGHT IN THE LONESOME OCTOBER

Author: **Richard Laymon**
Publisher: Leisure
Year of Publication: 2001
Genre: Horror / Thriller
Typology: Novel
Total Score: 88
Goodreads Score: 3,88

This is one of Laymon's most surreal and original novels. Here we follow the nocturnal walks of Ed Logan, a young student unwittingly setting out on an odyssey which will make him front row witness to the obscure lives of those who populate the night underground. These borderline characters, like hunters, wait for sunset to get to work—cannibals under bridges, ready to capture passers-by; violent sexual predators; a beautiful homeless woman who will teach Logan to embrace the wonders and terrors of the night; and the madwoman who rides her bicycle through the darkness. The novel unfolds in a series of dreams, tracking a vivid narrative that captures every last extreme detail. There is no lack of voyeurism, sex and violence here, characterized by the author's literary vision which perhaps makes this novel a little less slasher-oriented. This may seem atypical compared to Laymon's other works, but it certainly is no less interesting.

BEST 10 HORROR BOOKS FROM 1986 TO 2020
SELECTED BY

ELLEN DATLOW

THE SILENCE OF THE LAMBS by THOMAS HARRIS (1988)
GEEK LOVE by KATHERINE DUNN (1989)
THE CIPHER by KATHE KOJA (1991)
EXPOSURE by KATHRYN HARRISON (1993)
THROAT SPROCKETS by TIM LUCAS (1994)
A PRAYER FOR THE DYING by STEWART O'NAN (1999)
WORD MADE FLESH by JACK O'CONNELL (1999)
UNDER THE SKIN by MICHAEL FABER (2000)
GENERATION LOSS by ELIZABETH HAND (2007)
LET THE RIGHT ONE IN by JOHN AJVIDE LINDQVIST (2004)

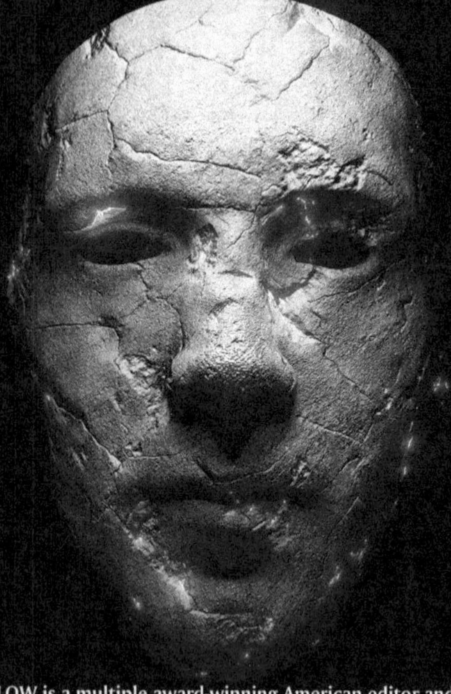

ELLEN DATLOW is a multiple award-winning American editor and anthologist. Among the over 100 anthologies she has edited are the well-known annual series *The Best Horror of the Year* (now in its 13th volume), *Lovecraft's Monsters* (2014); *Fearful Symmetries* (2014); *The Doll Collection* (2015), *The Monstrous* (2015), *Nightmares: A New Decade of Modern Horror* (2016), Black Feathers (2017), *The Devil and the Deep: Horror Stories of the Sea* (2018) and *Final Cuts: New Tales of Hollywood Horror and Other Spectacles* (2020).
Website: www.ellendatlow.com

NIGHT STONE

Author: **Rick Hautala**
Publisher: Zebra
Year of Publication: 1986
Genre: Horror
Typology: Novel
Total Score: 83
Goodreads Score: 3,73

A novel by an author who passed away prematurely, and is a recipient of the Bram Stoker Award for Lifetime Achievement. This work deals with classic themes like the haunted house and diabolical dolls. 12-year-old Beth and her family move to their ancestral home in Maine, originally belonging to the grandparents of her father, Don. Both the house and the surrounding woods have a bad reputation—and for good reason. Beth finds a strange handmade doll in a closet, which of course proves to be more than just a toy. But the discoveries (and events) which follow will be many, and ever more disturbing. Native American folklore takes its place in this narrative, recalling some works by King. A book full of suspense and claustrophobia, this one is recommended for fans of '80s horror.

NORTH AMERICAN LAKE MONSTERS

Author: **Nathan Ballingrud**
Publisher: Small Beer Press
Year of Publication: 2013
Genre: Horror
Typology: Story Collection
Total Score: 90
Goodreads Score: 4,00

This award-winning collection of short stories offers a roundup of monsters that, despite the title, have nothing to do with lake creatures. Ballingrud's monsters are often more human, showcasing personal demons that exist not in remote places or haunted houses, but in everyday life. There are also a few real creatures (werewolves, vampires) here, but they are not the common thread in this book. The author has defined the collection as 'stories of love and monsters', and in fact the explored themes deal with the complexity of human relationships. Among my favorite short stories are *The Crevasse* (co-written with Michael Bailey), *North American Lake Monsters, S.S.* and *The Way Station*. The author's prose is unconventional (much like his vision of the genre) but is nevertheless easily accessible to all readers.

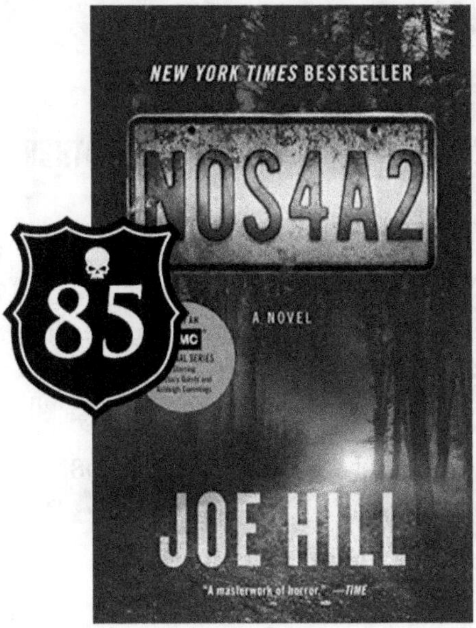

NOS4A2

Author: **Joe Hill**
Publisher: William Morrow
Year of Publication: 2013
Genre: Horror / Dark Fantasy
Typology: Novel
Total Score: 85
Goodreads Score: 4,08

This is the novel that in my opinion captures the best of the author, who stands independent of his famous father, Stephen King. In this black tale, it is possible for some to pass from the real world into a different dimension called 'Inscape', where the world of ideas is real. Among those able to enter this place we find Vic McQueen, who has the gift of finding lost things; Maggie Leigh, who can predict the future; and Charlie Manx who—with his 1938 Rolls Royce Wraith (license plate NOS4A2)—can transport children to an amazing and terrifying playground called Christmasland. But there is a price to pay for these 'gifts'. Manx experiences his ability differently, taking advantage of it like a vampire and absorbing the essence of his little passengers. A work between horror and dark fantasy, this disturbing tale deals with the themes of innocence, wonder and loss.

OCCULTATION AND OTHER STORIES

Author: **Laird Barron**
Publisher: Night Shade
Year of Publication: 2010
Genre: Horror / Weird
Typology: Story Collection
Total Score: 89
Goodreads Score: 4,08

This second collection from the author includes nine stories (and a novella) detailing the deeds of various characters who, outside of their normal lives, have to deal with a dark, chaotic world separate from their everyday personas. Here reality is merciless, devouring human frailties and reducing the characters to small voices lost within a malevolent chorus. This is weird fiction at its best, evoking visceral horror in settings which sometimes stand out more than the protagonists of the stories themselves. Among my favorites here include *30*, *Strappado*, the novella *Mysterium Tremendum* and *The Broadsword*. A book for keen readers of the genre.

ODD THOMAS

Author: **Dean Koontz**
Publisher: Bantam
Year of Publication: 2003
Genre: Horror / Thriller
Typology: Novel
Total Score: 86
Goodreads Score: 3,96

This novel tells the story of Odd Thomas, a young cook who has a psychic gift—or perhaps a curse: he sees the spirits of the dead, who come looking for him to communicate. Sometimes these souls seek justice, offering clues to help solve crimes (reported to the friendly police chief), or even to prevent them. But one day in Pico Mundo, a small town in California, a stranger appears—and everywhere he goes, a pack of dark spirits resembling hyenas follow. Though he senses that these shadows are a great threat, Thomas' supernatural informants can't help him this time. In the days that follow, catastrophe strikes the town and the young man, together with his girlfriend, Stormy, must race against time to counter the evil converging on the past, present and future. An exciting paranormal thriller with an original main character, this one is recommended for all readers.

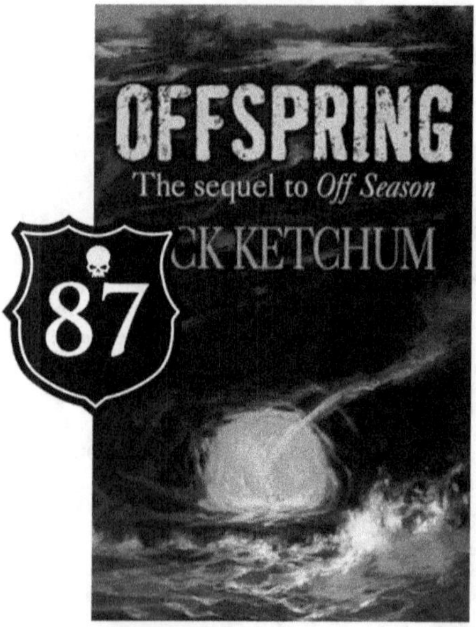

OFFSPRING

Author: **Jack Ketchum**
Publisher: Overlook Connection
Year of Publication: 1991
Genre: Horror
Typology: Novel
Total Score: 87
Goodreads Score: 3,79

This is the second of a trilogy which includes the preceding *Offseason* and later *The Woman*. This novel, crafted by one of the greatest masters of the genre, continues the story of the 'Family'—a tribe of savage cannibal predators—as they return to terrorize the coast of Maine: specifically to Dead River, a remote location and the scene of the previous massacre. The former Sheriff Peters, convinced he had solved the matter long ago, sees the nightmares that have long haunted him return in the flesh. Ketchum spares nothing from the start, describing brutality and cruelty with unflinching realism (though less than the first novel of the series) and great skill (showing the author's greater maturity). Suggested for fans of the darkest extremes.

BEST 10 HORROR BOOKS FROM 1986 TO 2020
SELECTED BY

STEVE RASNIC TEM

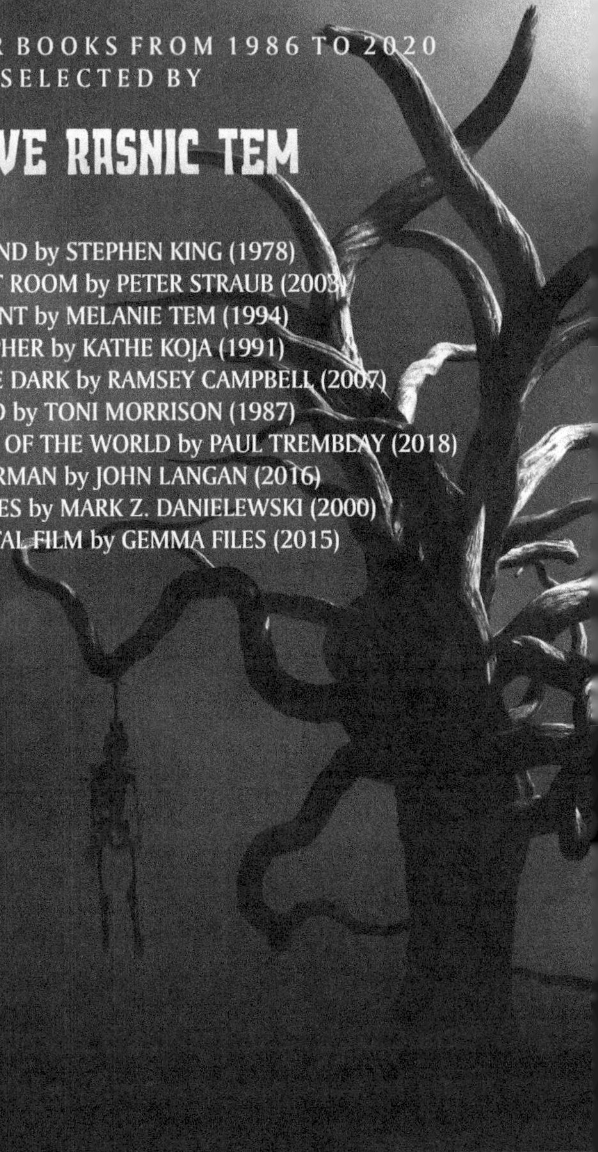

THE STAND by STEPHEN KING (1978)
IN THE NIGHT ROOM by PETER STRAUB (2003)
REVENANT by MELANIE TEM (1994)
THE CIPHER by KATHE KOJA (1991)
THE GRIN OF THE DARK by RAMSEY CAMPBELL (2007)
BELOVED by TONI MORRISON (1987)
THE CABIN AT THE END OF THE WORLD by PAUL TREMBLAY (2018)
THE FISHERMAN by JOHN LANGAN (2016)
HOUSE OF LEAVES by MARK Z. DANIELEWSKI (2000)
EXPERIMENTAL FILM by GEMMA FILES (2015)

STEVE RASNIC TEM is an award-winning American writer.
His works include *Excavation* (1986), *City Fishing* (2000), *The Book of Days* (2002), *The Man On The Ceiling* (2008, written with Melanie Tem), *Deadfall Hotel* (2012), *Celestial Inventories* (2013), *Blood Kin* (2014),*Ubo* (2017), *Figure Unseen* (2018), *The Night Doctor and Other Tales* (2019). Website: www.stevetem.com

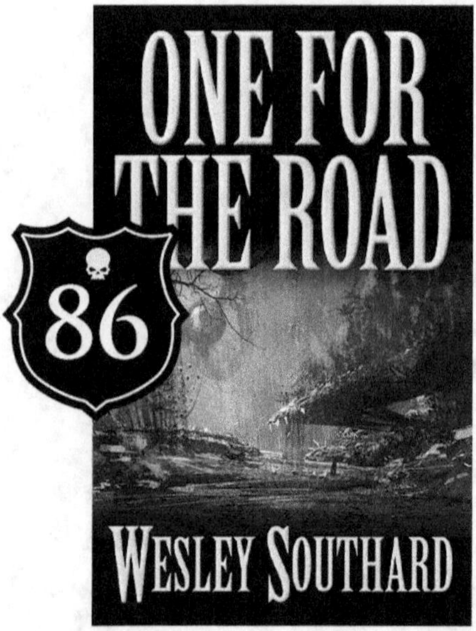

ONE FOR THE ROAD

Author: **Wesley Southard**
Publisher: Deadite
Year of Publication: 2019
Genre: Horror
Typology: Novella
Total Score: 86
Goodreads Score: 3,89

▶ This innovative novel takes us to a 'metal' version of hell. Ít's the last concert of the tour for the band Rot in Hell, and guitarist Spencer Hesston is looking forward to returning to the Midwest. But things aren't going to go as expected. The band, after traveling all night, wakes up dazed in the middle of the desert, finding themselves near an abandoned city. The landscape is hellish, animated by strange and surreal creatures. Raw storytelling, irony, fun, monsters and violence are at the core of this extravagant novel that does not take itself too seriously, and which recalls an inspired dark comedy in terms of structure and narrative philosophy. A very funny interpretation of cosmic horror set in a heavy metal frame.

OUT OF WATER

Author: **Sarah Read**
Publisher: Trepidatio Publishing
Year of Publication: 2019
Genre: Horror
Typology: Story Collection
Total Score: 86
Goodreads Score: 4,11

A fascinating collection of post-gothic short stories by the talented American author Sarah Read. These stories touch various themes, from loss to revenge, from pain to religious fanaticism, playing on the chessboard of the usual horror tropes, characterized (in addition to surreal 'buildings' and female characters) by a lyrical and refined prose. Among my favorite stories include *In Tongues*, *The Eyes of Salton Sea*, *Crosswind*, *Endoskeletal* and *Thorn Tongue*. Horror and beauty sometimes go very well together, as demonstrated by this dive into the dark waters of Sarah Read's imagination.

PANDEMONIUM

Author: **Daryl Gregory**
Publisher: Del Rey
Year of Publication: 2008
Genre: Horror / Thriller / Dark Fantasy
Typology: Novel
Total Score: 92
Goodreads Score: 3,82

Much like an outbreak or epidemic, in this novel the random phenomena of possession has beset the world. The entities or demons are born from the collective unconscious and archetypal behaviors of society. So we have the Painter, who leads people to create works of art; The Little Angel, who kills the sick by kissing them; the Captain, who possesses soldiers to incite heroic and lethal actions; the Truth, who kills those who lie; and many others. But there's more in this amazing book. The main character, Del (possessed as a child), doesn't know if there is still something inside him or someone in the depths of his consciousness, and he decides to look for answers. An exciting, dark book, simultaneously nostalgic and fun with an innovative take on the classic theme of possession. This work combines a very effective dark fantasy/SciFi atmosphere and three-dimensional characters with a hefty dose of sarcasm.

PEACEABLE KINGDOM

Author: **Jack Ketchum**
Publisher: Leisure
Year of Publication: 2003
Genre: Horror / Thriller
Typology: Story Collection
Total Score: 88
Goodreads Score: 3,89

An eclectic collection of 32 short stories (published from 1994 to 2003) by Jack Ketchum, transcending the boundaries of horror and interpreting multiple genres and themes to display all the skills of this great author. Among the stories I liked the most are *The Work*, *The Rifle*, *The Box*, *The Haunt*, *Megan's Law*, *Redemption* and *Gone*. These are harrowing, dark and disturbing stories in which human horror almost always prevails over the supernatural. In fact the supernatural barely appears in this book—but that doesn't apply only to this collection, as real-world horror is a trademark of the author. Ketchum evokes in the reader a range of strong, often contradictory emotions: fear, disgust, cruelty and courage. There is certainly no lack of brutality, blood and sex, even if these make fewer appearances here as compared with the author's novels. There are several pearls in this collection, each of which would on its own make this book worth the read, even among the few less-inspired pieces.

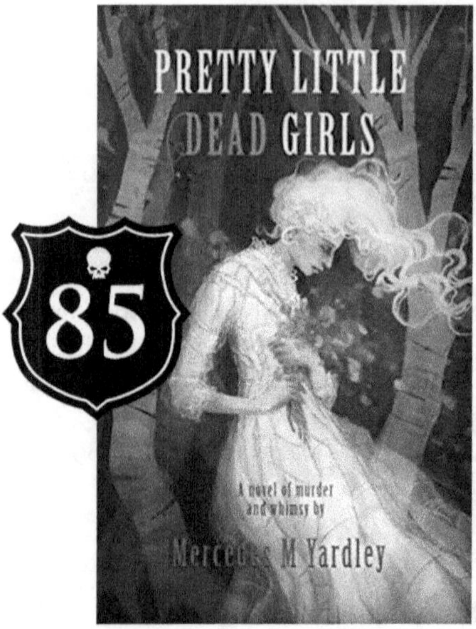

PRETTY LITTLE DEAD GIRLS

Author: **Mercedes Murdock Yardley**
Publisher: Ragnarok
Year of Publication: 2014
Genre: Horror / Dark Fantasy
Typology: Novel
Total Score: 85
Goodreads Score: 3,95

An original novel by one of the most interesting and gifted new interpreters of the genre. The protagonist, Bryony Adams, is destined to be killed, and to die young. This is known to us from the first page of the book. She knows it, and everyone around her knows it too. She lives her life waiting for her fate to befall her. Wherever she goes, people die—as if she is being chased by death, which repeatedly fails to hit its intended target. The story is therefore centered on the awareness of a brief life and the emotions of loved ones who share the knowledge of this 'shortened' journey. Despite this obscure premise where the end is already given, this novel affirms life through the author's joyful and lively prose, which collides with the disturbing atmosphere of the book. A dark and very original fairy tale with dark fantasy elements, this mature story explores the intricacies of destiny, death, beauty, personal relationships, everyday life and extravagance.

REINCARNAGE

Author: **Ryan Harding and Jason Taverner**
Publisher: Deadite
Year of Publication: 2015
Genre: Horror / Splatterpunk / Slasher
Typology: Novel
Total Score: 87
Goodreads Score 3,99

Ryan Harding (here with Jason Taverner) is one of the leading interpreters of contemporary extreme horror. In this novel he presents us with an appealing main character, a former Vietnam veteran called 'Agent Orange' who has not only become a brutal serial killer, but is also indestructible. If someone kills him, he comes back to life. The government, desperate to quench the thirst of this supernatural predator, has locked him up in a secure area surrounding Morgan Falls (a wilderness fortress, essentially a game reserve), providing him with victims from time to time. The story tells the fates of some of those victims, and their fight to survive. The content here is strong (but there is no lack of irony), and the author portrays each bloodbath in unflinching detail, including eviscerations, beheadings, strangulations with the entrails, scalpings with machetes, and many other atrocities. A tribute to the '80s slasher movie which fans of the genre are sure to enjoy, this is not recommended for all readers.

BEST 10 HORROR ESSAYS
SELECTED AND COMMENTED BY
LISA MORTON

BEST 10 HORROR ESSAYS

SELECTED AND COMMENTED BY LISA MORTON

On the Supernatural in Poetry by Ann Radcliffe, The New Monthly Magazine, 1826. "Terror and horror are so far opposite, that the first expands the soul, and awakens the faculties to a high degree of life; the other contracts, freezes, and nearly annihilates them." This piece was cut from Radcliffe's Gothic masterpiece *The Mysteries of Udolpho* and published posthumously. It begins with a lengthy discussion of Shakespeare's use of the supernatural, but the eventual discussion of horror versus terror is still quoted and studied 200 years later.

A Christmas Tree by Charles Dickens, 1850. "There is no end to the old houses, with resounding galleries, and dismal state–bedchambers, and haunted wings shut up for many years, through which we may ramble, with an agreeable creeping up our back, and encounter any number of ghosts, but (it is worthy of remark perhaps) reducible to a very few general types and classes; for, ghosts have little originality, and 'walk' in a beaten track." Don't let the first half of this essay by the author of the greatest ghost story ever written fool you—yes, it's about his memories of Christmas as a child. But the second half is a survey of themes common in horror fiction at the time, retold in Dickens' inimitable style.

The Decay of the British Ghost by F. Anstey, in Longmans Magazine, January 1884. "There was something thoroughly Christmassy, for example, about the witchlike old lady, with a horrible dead rouged face, who looked out of a tarnished mirror and gibbered malevolently." Although this essay was intended as a snarky send-up of ghosts in both real life and fiction, it provides some useful insights into the nineteenth-century ghost story, talking about the ghost story's ubiquity in Christmas issues of magazines, and how the widespread fakery of mediums at the time might have damaged public interest in ghosts overall.

Supernatural Horror in Literature by H.P. Lovecraft, The Recluse, August 1927. "The oldest and strongest emotion of mankind is fear, and the oldest and strongest kind of fear is fear of the unknown. These facts few psychologists will dispute, and their admitted truth must establish for all time the genuineness and dignity of the weirdly horrible tale as a literary form." Regardless of how one feels about Lovecraft's fiction or the man himself, the importance of this overview of the horror genre up to 1927 is undeniable.

Some Remarks on Ghost Stories by M.R. James, The Bookman, December 1929. "The reading of many ghost stories has shown me that the greatest successes have been scored by the authors who can make us envisage a definite time and place, and give us plenty of clear-cut and matter-of-fact detail, but who, when the climax is reached, allow us to be just a little in the dark as to the working of their machinery." Possibly the greatest practitioner of ghost stories provides an overview of the genre as he knew it in 1929, drawing a line from Shakespeare through Poe and Dickens to Le Fanu and E. F. Benson.

Her Body, Himself: Gender in the Slasher Film by Carol J. Clover, Representations Autumn 1987. "The image of the distressed female most likely to linger in memory is the image of the one who did not die: the survivor, or Final Girl." Published five years before her seminal book *Men, Women, and Chainsaws: Gender in the Modern Horror Film*, this essay gave the world the term "Final Girl" and is a significant dissection of how gender worked in horror of the 1970s and 1980s

Introduction to Prime Evil by Douglas E. Winter, 1988. "Horror is not a genre, it is an emotion. It is a progressive form of fiction, one that evolves to meet the fears and anxieties of its times." More than 30 years after it was written, Winter's introductory essay to his anthology *Prime Evil* still engenders debate and discussion—*is* horror a genre?

Magic, Madness, and Women Who Creep: The Power of Individuality in the Work of Charlotte Perkins Gilman by Gwendolyn Kiste, Vastarien: A Literary Journal Vol. 2, Issue 1, 2019. "When examining Gilman's legacy, it could be easy and a little facile to choose one of her roles over the other as her predominant identity: namely, either Gilman the horror and fantasy author or Gilman the activist. Perhaps, though, the two sides are not so fragmented." Not only did Kiste win the first Bram Stoker Award® for Short Non-fiction for this piece, she stands at the forefront of a new wave of female writers and scholars who are re-examining the genre's history with a special emphasis on the role that women authors, authors of color, and LGBTQ authors may have played.

Introduction to The New Annotated H.P. Lovecraft: Beyond Arkham by Victor LaValle, 2019. "You can love something, love someone, *and* criticize them. That's called maturity." The finest Black author of weird fiction gets personal here, discussing the influence of Lovecraft on him, his shock at unearthing Lovecraft's racism, and his solution for reconciling the genre's past with the present.

Horror, Personality and Threat Simulation: A Survey on the Psychology of Scary Media by Mathias Clasen, Jens Kjeldgaard-Christiansen and John A. Johnson, Evolutionary Behavioral Sciences, July 2020. "While frightening media may be initially aversive, people high in sensation seeking and intellect/imagination, in particular, like intellectual stimulation and challenge and expect not just negative but also positive emotions from horror consumption." Although it's hard to choose just one work from Clasen's prolific output, this paper is a good look at why he's one of the most important academics in the field of horror today: he doesn't just describe frightening things, he tells us exactly why we find them frightening, down to our physiological responses.

LISA MORTON

Lisa Morton. American writer, screenwriter, essayist and editor, she has won the Bram Stoker Award six times and is the former President of the Horror Writers Association. Her non-fiction works include: *The Halloween Encyclopedia* (2003); *A Hallowe'en Anthology: Literary and Historical Writings Over the Centuries* (2008): *Trick or Treat: A Hystory of Halloween* (2012); *Ghost: A Haunted History; Calling the Spirits: A Hystory of Seances* (2020).
Website: **www.lisamorton.com**

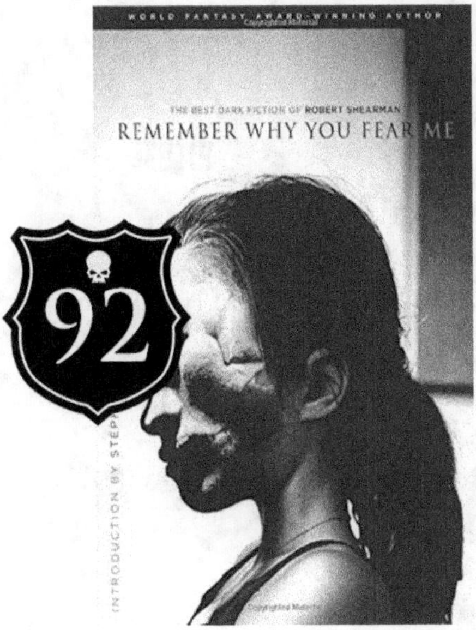

REMEMBER WHY YOU FEAR ME

Author: **Robert Shearman**
Publisher: ChiZine
Year of Publication: 2012
Genre: Horror / Weird
Typology: Story Collection
Total Score: 92
Goodreads Score: 4,04

A collection of the best short stories (including four excellent bonus novelettes) by Robert Shearman, a great interpreter of all round dark/weird genres and the maker of surreal nightmares who sometimes reminds us of Neil Gaiman. Here a man suspects that the face of his dead wife is growing over his own; another man goes to hell and discovers that he shares a room with Hitler's dog; a haunted house stands in the center of the Garden of Eden. Other stories tell of murderous angels and a woman who gives birth to a sofa. This is literary, psychological, social horror. Among my favorite stories are *A Good Grief*; *Damned If You Don't*; *The Bathtub*; *In the Dark Space*; *Blue Crayon, Yellow Crayon*; and *Pang*. In my opinion, this is the best book for a reader to get to know this brilliant author.

RITUAL

Author: **Graham Masterton**
Publisher: Time Warner
Year of Publication: 1988
Genre: Horror / Thriller
Typology: Novel
Total Score: 85
Goodreads Score: 3,77

Charlie McLean, a restaurant guide critic who travels constantly, goes with his son Martin to the town of Allen's Corner in rural Connecticut to visit an exclusive French restaurant called *Le Repoisoir*. This place has an unconventional menu (yep, we are talking about human flesh) and it turns out to also be a sort of secret society. First, the two are not permitted access. Then the critic's son mysteriously disappears. Bloody like the works of Ketchum or Laymon—and so not for delicate stomachs—Masterton develops the theme of cannibalism in a different way than usual, linking it to a bizarre and vast cult which holds particular purposes and philosophies (there is a Savior involved, like in all self-respecting religions). Between horror and thriller and with a good dose of suspense, this is a visceral work quite typical of Masterton's large production style, and presents a sinister ending.

SCARS AND OTHER DISTINGUISHING MARKS

Author: **Richard Christian Matheson**
Publisher: Tor Books
Year of Publication: 1987
Genre: Psychological Horror / Magic Realism / Dark Fantasy
Typology: Story Collection
Total Score: 88
Goodreads Score: 3,72

This is the first collection of (27) short stories by Richard Christian Matheson, writer and screenwriter. The son of Richard Matheson (author of the famous *I Am Legend*), the younger Matheson is an equally illustrious and original artist. The genre here is not easily categorised, as these stories are a mix of noir, psychological horror, thriller, magic realism and dark fantasy. The short length (and effectiveness) of the stories—together with his lyrical, minimalist style—is characteristic of Richard Christian Matheson, who excels in this narrative field and stands among its best interpreters. This is a book for everyone. Heterogeneous in terms of themes, the collection includes stand-out stories like *Red*, *Vampire*, *Graduation* and *Goosebumps*, with introductions by Stephen King and Dennis Etchison.

SKIDDING INTO OBLIVION

Author: **Brian Hodge**
Publisher: ChiZine
Year of Publication: 2019
Genre: Horror / Weird
Typology: Story Collection
Total Score: 92
Goodreads Score: 4,26

This is the fifth (and very inspired) horror/weird collection from this author. While some of these stories show the 'social' roots of horror by innovating the sub-themes, they also give new life to the visions of a master like Lovecraft through effective reinterpretations. Among these include *The Same Deep Waters as You*, *One Possible Shape of Things to Come*, *One Last Year Without Summer* and *The Stagnant Breath of Change*. These tales in particular are not to be missed by fans. With great control of prose and boundless imagination, Hodge guides us along the invisible boundary between dreams and reality.

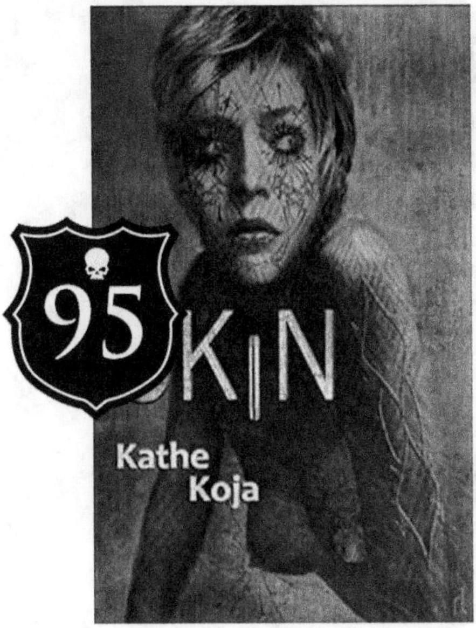

SKIN

Author: **Kathe Koja**
Publisher: Dell
Year of Publication: 1993
Genre: Horror / Weird
Typology: Novel
Total Score: 95
Goodreads Score: 3,81

Kathe Koja is one of the most original and provocative voices in contemporary horror, transcending the boundaries of the genre and expanding on some of Barker's visions. Tess Bajac spends her days collecting fragments of material for her strange metal sculptures. Bibi, on the other hand, is a dancer/performer, and she carves the muscles and skin (see: scarification) of her own body. The two women, immersed in their obsessions, join to create a new form of art: a show of metal and flesh. But like an addiction, the soul of everything is represented by a pain which demands more and more. The streamlined, postmodern prose is unconventional, at times itself becoming experimental art in good keeping with the book. This one will be appreciated by discerning readers who expect more than mere entertainment from their horror fiction. Extreme art, creation, destruction, transcendence: this is a book I could define as a cult classic of 'underground' horror.

SLOB

Author: **Rex Miller**
Publisher: Ereads
Year of Publication: 1987
Genre: Horror / Splatterpunk / Thriller
Typology: Novel
Total Score: 84
Goodreads Score: 3,44

Rex Miller's debut novel tells the story of a psychopath—a born murderer gifted with precognition—called Chaingang, who identifies himself with death itself, and leaves a trail of carnage everywhere behind him. Detective Eichord of the Chicago Police Department (who struggles with alcoholism) will try to stop Chaingang by studying the mind of a hunter: a real killing machine. A work with brutal content (violence, cannibalism, rape) which can be partly categorized as splatterpunk (although it is missing some of the subversive social themes typical of the movement), some elements of crime fiction are also present here. The prose is fast and engaging, framed in the genre vision of the '80s. A book for genre fans, this is not recommended for readers who don't appreciate graphic content.

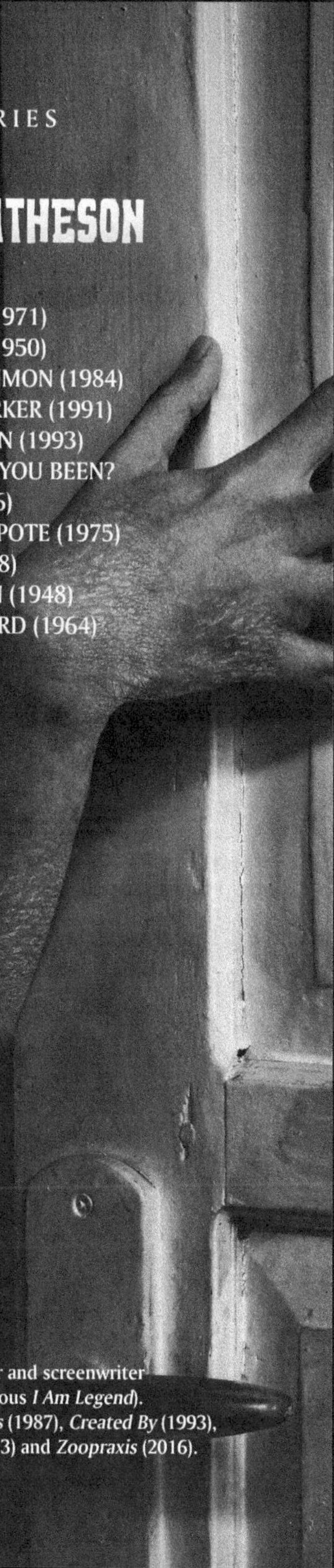

BEST 10 HORROR STORIES
SELECTED BY

RICHARD CHRISTIAN MATHESON

DUEL by RICHARD MATHESON (1971)
THE VELDT by RAY BRADBURY (1950)
NIGHTCRAWLERS by ROBERT R. MCCAMMON (1984)
IN THE HILLS, THE CITIES by CLIVE BARKER (1991)
THE DOG PARK by DENNIS ETCHISON (1993)
WHERE ARE YOU GOING, WHERE HAVE YOU BEEN?
by JOYCE CAROL OATES (1966)
HANDCARVED COFFINS by TRUMAN CAPOTE (1975)
NONA by STEPHEN KING (1978)
THE LOTTERY by SHIRLEY JACKSON (1948)
THE DROWNED GIANT by J. G. BALLARD (1964)

RICHARD CHRISTIAN MATHESON is an American writer and screenwriter and is the son of Richard Matheson (author of the famous *I Am Legend*). His fiction works include *Scars and other Distinguishable Marks* (1987), *Created By* (1993), *Dystopia: Collected Stories* (2000), *The Ritual of Illusions* (2013) and *Zoopraxis* (2016).

SOFT APOCALYPSES

Author: **Lucy A. Snyder**
Publisher: Raw Dog Screaming Press
Year of Publication: 2014
Genre: Horror / Dark Fantasy
Typology: Story Collection
Total Score: 86
Goodreads Score: 3,91

In this collection of 15 short stories ranging between horror and dark fantasy, and raiding steampunk and post apocalyptic science fiction, Snyder proves to be by far one of the best contemporary interpreters of the genre. While dark and brutal, these stories maintain a high standard in intense, engaging prose. Some interesting reworkings of classic tropes such as zombies and vampires are introduced here, and human cruelty is also brought to light between these pages. Among my favorite stories are *Antumbra*, *Magdala Amygdala*, *Spare the Rod* and *The Leviathan of Trincomalee*.

SONG FOR THE UNRAVELING OF THE WORLD

Author: **Brian Evenson**
Publisher: Coffee House Press
Year of Publication: 2019
Genre: Horror / Weird
Typology: Story Collection
Total Score: 89
Goodreads Score: 3,89

Few short story collections deserve the degree of attention this author's consistently do. Evenson's stories, in their timeless settings, often converge on ordinary people thrown into disturbing situations via horror and science fiction tropes. Evenson's brilliant minimalist prose mixes different styles and is never predictable, a formula which is highly effective in drawing the reader into the dark folds of distorted reality and human fragility. Existentialism and subconscious understanding work like shadows, skilfully guided by the author. This is a book for everyone, but especially those who prefer quiet unease over horror held in plain sight. Among my favorite stories are *The Tower*, *Smear*, *Lather of Flies* and *Line of Sight*.

SOURDOUGH AND OTHER STORIES

Author: **Angela Slatter**
Publisher: Tartarus Press
Year of Publication: 2010
Genre: Dark Fantasy
Typology: Story Collection
Total Score: 88
Goodreads Score: 4,54

A collection of 16 dark fantasy stories and dark fairy tales by Australian author Angela Slatter. Here witches, ghosts, spirits and magic revolve around the female universe, with characters (including a reimagining of Rapunzel) floating on the edges of the real world. These stories are interconnected, making the book a sort of novel. Slatter's clear prose is engaging and offers a three-dimensionality to the characters and their unique psychologies. Including this book in this guide is something of an exception, given the genre to which this work belongs (oriented towards fantasy rather than horror), but dark fairy tales in my opinion are an important relative of horror, and this book deserves to be read by genre fans. Recommended for fans of this kind of fiction (and of the Brothers Grimm).

83

SUFFER THE FLESH

Author: **Monica J. O'Rourke**
Publisher: Prime Books
Year of Publication: 2002
Genre: Extreme / Hardcore Horror
Typology: Short Novel
Total Score: 83
Goodreads Score: 3,48

The first novel from an author who will soon became one of the favorites among splatterpunk and extreme horror fans. This raw and violent book tells the story of Zoey Masterson, a lonely and overweight woman who finds herself in the hands of dark, crazy people who take her into a seedy nightmare world, claiming that it is for her own good. Holding her in a bunker, their method of weight loss is to rape, humiliate and torture her through various degrading sexual acts. Zoey will have to learn to survive these daily perversions. Reminiscent of the works of the Marquis De Sade—but also of historical atrocities committed against women, such as the 17th century witch trials—this story manages to hide a few twists. Suffering and the psychological trauma associated with rape are the guiding stars of this novel. Given the extreme content, this one is suggested only for fans of the genre. The twisted visions of J.F. Gonzalez are one step away.

SURVIVOR

Author: **J.F. Gonzalez**
Publisher: Dorchester
Year of Publication: 2004
Genre: Extreme / Hardcore Horror
Typology: Novel
Total Score: 89
Goodreads Score: 3,86

Lisa is ready to spend a romantic weekend with her husband, and she can't wait to tell him she's expecting a baby. But the program that Gonzalez, a great master of extreme horror, has in mind for her is quite different. The story quickly turns into a nightmare for Lisa when her husband is arrested and she is kidnapped. But there's no ransom—Lisa is destined to become the star of a snuff movie. Similar to some works by Ketchum, the horror here is purely human (no arcane creatures or supernatural enemies required) and the monsters are depraved psychopaths. Expect the worst atrocities—this book is a ticket to a sick, sadistic journey into the hell of pornography. This novel is considered (rightly) one of the highest peaks reached by hardcore/extreme horror, and is only for fans of the genre. If you are among them, this one is truly not to be missed.

SWAN SONG

Author: **Robert R. McCammon**
Publisher: Pocket Books
Year of Publication: 1987
Genre: Horror
Typology: Novel
Total Score: 91
Goodreads Score 4,28

A mighty, dense novel by a great master of the genre, this one is close to McCammon's best. An inspired interpretation of the horror/post-apocalyptic subgenre, the story is set in the 1980s, in the wasteland of a nuclear holocaust. The paths of various characters intertwine: Josh, a traveling wrestler; Sue Wanda, called Swan, who has the power to give life to things; Sister Creep, a madwoman who lives on the street; and Roland, a teenager who is a zealous member of the predatory Army of Excellence. But perhaps the Devil himself also stalks the wasteland . . . along with other strange, monstrous creatures. The last survivors on Earth are dragged into an epic battle between good and evil, between those who want to rebuild the world and those wanting to plunder what is left, giving free rein to violence. If you liked King's *The Stand*, then make this book yours. A novel for everyone.

BEST 10 HORROR BOOKS FROM 1986 TO 2020
SELECTED BY

DAVID J. SCHOW

WILDWOOD by JOHN FARRIS (1986)
ANGRY CANDY by HARLAN ELLISON (1988)
FLICKER by THEODORE ROSZAK (1991)
PSYCHO-PATHS Edited by ROBERT BLOCH (1991)
THE GOLDEN by LUCIUS SHEPARD (2013)
MAGIC TERROR by PETER STRAUB (2000)
SMOKE GHOST & OTHER APPARITIONS by FRITZ LEIBER (2002)
SCARED STIFF: TALES OF SEX AND DEATH
by RAMSEY CAMPBELL (1987)
HAUNTED by CHUCK PALAHNIUK (2005)
THE TERROR by DAN SIMMONS (2007)

DAVID J. SCHOW is an American writer and editor, and is one of the original creators of the Splatterpunk movement. His novels include *The Kill Riff* (1988), *Lost Angels* (1990), *The Shaft* (1990), *Black Leather Required* (1994), *Crypt of Orchids* (1998), *Upgunned* (2012), *DJ Stories: The Best of David J. Schow* (2018) and *Monster Movies* (2020).

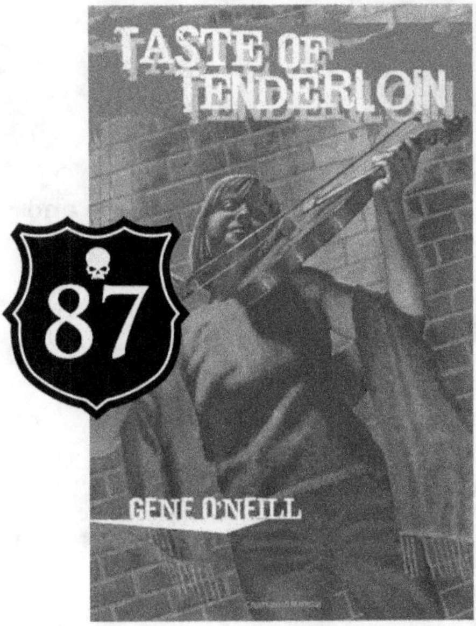

TASTE OF TENDERLOIN

Author: **Gene O'Neill**
Publisher: Apex
Year of Publication: 2009
Genre: Horror / Dark Fantasy
Typology: Story Collection
Total Score: 87
Goodreads Score: 3,94

A collection of eight stories straddling horror and dark fantasy guides us through the Tenderloin neighborhood of San Francisco. Portrayed as a surreal mouth, the city swallows dreams, lives, and the secrets and sins of its inhabitants. Each story—which combines fantastic elements with a raw and dark realism—presents varied characters including prostitutes, drug addicts, alcoholics, former boxers and war veterans; in short, these stories capture many lost souls, each well characterized by this great author. Among my favorite short stories include *Tombstones in His Eyes*, *Balance* and *Bruised Souls*. A book recommended for everyone, not only genre fans.

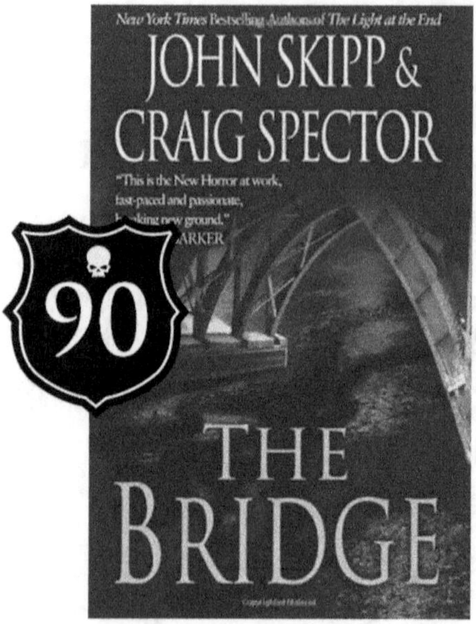

THE BRIDGE

Author: **John Skipp and Craig Spector**
Publisher: Spectra
Year of Publication: 1991
Genre: Horror / Splatterpunk
Typology: Novel
Total Score: 90
Goodreads Score: 3,63

In Paradise, Pennsylvania, entrepreneurs and authorities don't mind ignoring environmental protection laws to make a profit. Paradise Waste Disposal, a contaminated waste disposal facility, entrusts the surplus to Pusser's Scrap & Salvage, happy to make money by illegally dumping waste across the county. The Black Bridge, a dilapidated railway bridge over the Codorus stream, thus becomes a real chemical sewer. During a stormy night, Boonie and Drew Pusser throw a load of toxic sewage from their truck off the bridge. The die is cast. From this 'primordial soup' a new life is born, one capable of changing living cells, animating inert objects and regenerating the dead. Original and brilliant, this interpretation of ecological horror by the well-known splatterpunk duo is still highly topical almost 30 years after its publication.

THE CARP-FACED BOY AND OTHER TALES

Author: **Thersa Matsuura**
Publisher: Independent Legions
Year of Publication: 2017
Genre: Horror / Dark Fantasy / Weird
Typology: Story Collection
Total Score: 92
Goodreads Score: 4,30

A collection of stories by an American author who spent many years living in a fishing village in Japan, these tales are steeped with fascinating Japanese folklore in its great tradition of the fantastic. Matsuura's original, intense prose is fresh and modern, offering something unique in the horror and dark fantasy landscape. This interpretation of the genre touches on magic realism and leaves plenty of room for bizarre imagination over more naked, raw horror. Among my favorite stories include *Spider Sweeper*, *Mother of All Devils*, *Four Guys Walk Into a Bar* and *The Carp-Faced Boy*. A book recommended for everyone.

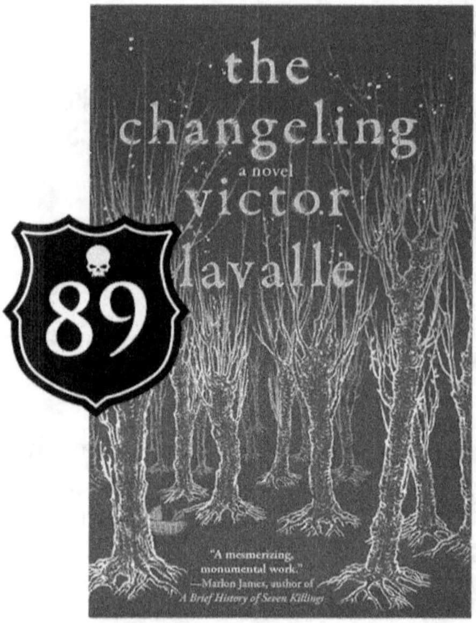

THE CHANGELING

Author: **Victor LaValle**
Publisher: Spiegel & Grau
Year of Publication: 2017
Genre: Dark Fantasy
Typology: Novel
Total Score: 89
Goodreads Score: 3,79

A novel from one of the most lauded voices of the contemporary fantastic. Apollo Kagwa, a book merchant and passionate reader with a Ugandan mother and a tough childhood behind him, becomes a father. Unlike his father who abandoned him, Apollo has a strong resolve to take an active role in the life of his son, Brian—but then his wife (librarian Emma) begins to behave strangely with the baby, distancing herself from him. Postpartum depression? Not really—it seems this situation goes way beyond the norm. Emma disappears shortly after committing a horrific act, and so begins Apollo's journey to find her and uncover the truth. This is the moment when the author introduces fantastic places and creatures into this story, giving life to a modern black fairy tale where technology plays an important part. LaValle explores various themes with great originality: fatherhood, responsibility, family, the use of social media, racism and immigration.

THE COLLECTION

Author: **Bentley Little**
Publisher: Signed Book
Year of Publication: 2002
Genre: Horror
Typology: Story Collection
Total Score: 88
Goodreads Score: 3,93

This collection of 32 tales by a genre master offers all flavors of dark fiction with great breadth, vision and skill. Little presents us with stories that mix horror, the absurd and the surreal with brutality and suspense. As always, the author is as generous with the blood spilling as he is careful to develop the social themes in his stories. A talented voice genre fans cannot miss, his ability to focus on any idea (simple, conventional or completely pedestrian) and turn it into a conduit for dread and unease is reminiscent only of Stephen King. Among my favorite stories include *Estoppel*, *The Washingtonians* (a crazy, must-read piece), *The Man in the Passenger Seat*, *Life With Father* and *The Idol.*

BEST 10 HORROR STORIES
PUBLISHED IN SPACE AND TIME MAGAZINE (2019/2020)
SELECTED BY

ANGELA YURIKO SMITH

COLLECTION VIOLET by AUSTIN CRAGG (Issue 138, 2020)
THE DEAD DON'T DREAM by GORDON LINTZNER (Issue 138, 2020)
ARTIFACT by JONATHAN MABERRY (Issue 137, 2020)
JOY OF LIFE by ALESSANDRO MANZETTI (Issue 137, 2020)
IN THE GLASS DARKLY by IAN ROGERS (Issue 134, 2019)
HANDS OF A TOOLMAKER by ERIC DEL CARLO (Issue 135, 2019)
A FAREWELL TO WORMS by JOHN LINKWOOD GRANT (Issue 134, 2019)
HUMANI by JOHN PALISANO (Issue 134, 2019)
THE FELINE, THE WITCH AND THE UNIVERSE
by JENNIFER SHELBY (Issue 135, 2019)

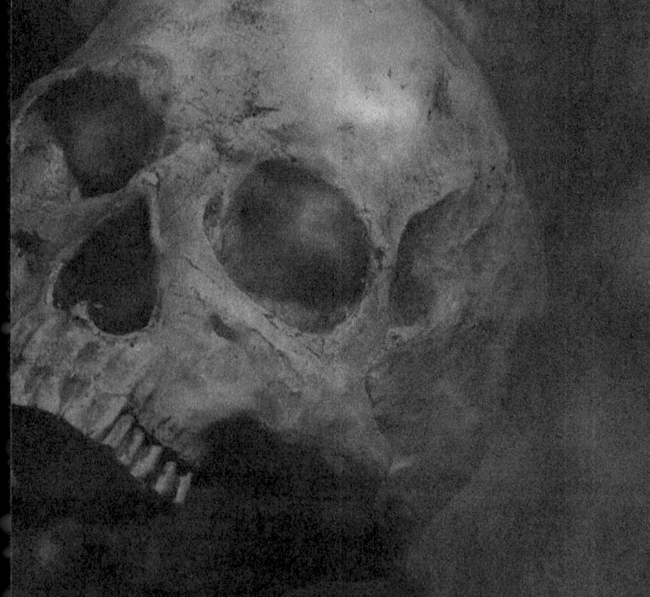

ANGELA YURIKO SMITH is an American writer and editor, and is the Editor-in-Chief of Space and Time Magazine. Among her works of fiction and poetry are *End of Mae* (2012), *Mr. Bonejangles and Other Tales of Dark Karma* (2015), *In Favor of Pain* (2016), *Escape Claws* (2017), *Bitter Suites* (2018), *Altars and Oubliettes* (2020) and *Suite and Sour* (2020).
Website: www.angelaysmith.com

THE CONQUEROR WORMS

Author: **Brian Keene**
Publisher: Leisure
Year of Publication: 2005
Genre: Horror / Dark Fantasy
Typology: Novel
Total Score: 88
Goodreads Score 3,88

One of the best novels by Brian Keene, another big name in the schlock subgenre. The story begins in the midst of a catastrophic flood that has overwhelmed entire cities. Here we are introduced to Teddy Garnett, a sprightly old man who doesn't want to leave his home at the top of the Appalachian mountains. He is the only human still alive in the small community of Punkin 'Center, now reduced to an islet. But when Teddy receives a visit from Carl, his best friend believed to be dead, he discovers that there are worse things going on than the rain. There are creatures underground . . . and they have begun to dig towards the surface, intent on conquering the world. But there are still more surprises coming, and something big—with Lovecraftian levels of blood—will rise. This novel offers a creative vision of the end of the world, and its second half throws us into pure action that propels us to the end at a frenzied pace.

THE DEATH ARTIST

Author: **Dennis Etchison**
Publisher: Leisure
Year of Publication: 2000
Genre: Horror
Typology: Story Collection
Total Score: 87
Goodreads Score: 3,55

A collection of 12 short stories by another renowned genre artist who has unfortunately passed away. Etchison's stories (which excel in short form) are original and ambiguous, with surrealist tones, and they know how to get under the reader's skin and stay there for a long time. His use of the 'unspoken', much like dream logic, is often very effective in stimulating the reader's imagination and allowing unease to flourish between the lines. The *fil rouge* in these tales is the location, Los Angeles, rather than any clear recurring themes. Among my favorite stories are *The Last Reel*, *When They Gave us Memory* and *Inside the Cackle Factory*.

THE DEVIL IN GRAY

Author: **Graham Masterton**
Publisher: Leisure
Year of Publication: 2004
Genre: Horror / Thriller
Typology: Novel
Total Score: 87
Goodreads Score: 3,79

This novel works off a strange combination: Santeria and the American Civil War. A mysterious man (or entity) perpetrates several heinous and bizarre murders. He's not alive, but he's not dead either, and he looks like a former Confederate soldier. Is he a bloodthirsty, immortal spirit seeking revenge? Did he ever really exist in human flesh, once upon a time? These are the questions that run through the reader's mind in this book by Masterton, who—with his solid realism—once again brings folklore (in this case, Santeria) into play. The protagonist of the story is Detective Decker, who will have to hunt down the demon in gray. But he will need help. Hedging between horror and the paranormal, the author keeps us gripped all the way to the stunning conclusion.

THE DIVINITY STUDENT

Author: **Michael Cisco**
Publisher: Buzzcity Press
Year of Publication: 1999
Genre: Weird / Dark Fantasy
Typology: Novel
Total Score: 92
Goodreads Score: 3,84

A surrealist weird/dark fantasy novel imbued with magic realism. This fascinating writer captures a mesmerizing atmosphere made even more original by his unconventional prose and story structures. Set in the labyrinthine city of San Veneficio, the main character in this story remains unnamed throughout. We initially meet him while he is in the process of evisceration, after which he is stuffed with the pages of sacred books and immersed in water. Following this ritual, he is brought back to life by strange creatures. His destiny as a new 'Golem' is to become a secret 'word seeker'. His path ahead will be unpredictable, and knowledge will merge with madness along the way. A beautiful exploration into the power of words, this book is a must-have for discerning readers. It is otherwise not for everyone, given the complexity of the abstract, dreamlike and almost hallucinogenic vision evoked by Cisco's refined style.

THE DROWNING GIRL

Author: **Caitlín R. Kiernan**
Publisher: Roc
Year of Publication: 2012
Genre: Dark Fantasy
Typology: Novel
Total Score: 94
Goodreads Score: 3,71

An award-winning weird/dark fantasy novel by one of the greatest (and most gifted) interpreters of modern and contemporary fantastic fiction. The protagonist of this original, hypnotic ghost story *sui generis* is India Morgan Phelps, called Imp by her friends, a schizophrenic artist who cannot trust her own mind. The sophisticated narrative uses parallel timelines (and dimensions), and the story's supernatural happenings are told to us by the same protagonist. In her distorted perception of reality, these events acquire different meanings and symbolisms—a search for the truth which leads to encounters with sirens, werewolves, and lost and found lovers. A staging of human consciousness of literary value which skillfully weaves the transparent threads of psychology and the supernatural, this one is highly recommended for discerning readers.

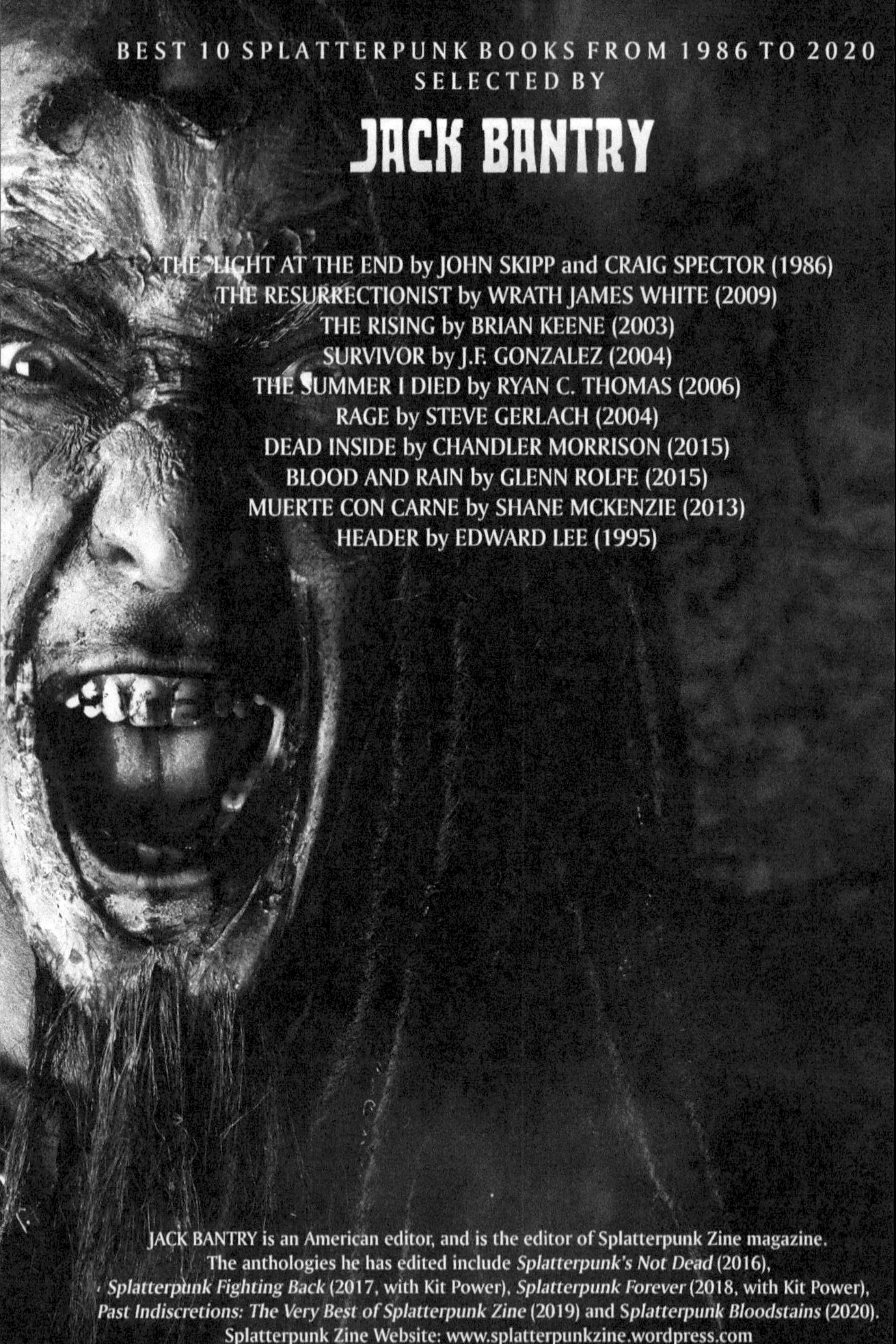

BEST 10 SPLATTERPUNK BOOKS FROM 1986 TO 2020
SELECTED BY

JACK BANTRY

THE LIGHT AT THE END by JOHN SKIPP and CRAIG SPECTOR (1986)
THE RESURRECTIONIST by WRATH JAMES WHITE (2009)
THE RISING by BRIAN KEENE (2003)
SURVIVOR by J.F. GONZALEZ (2004)
THE SUMMER I DIED by RYAN C. THOMAS (2006)
RAGE by STEVE GERLACH (2004)
DEAD INSIDE by CHANDLER MORRISON (2015)
BLOOD AND RAIN by GLENN ROLFE (2015)
MUERTE CON CARNE by SHANE MCKENZIE (2013)
HEADER by EDWARD LEE (1995)

JACK BANTRY is an American editor, and is the editor of Splatterpunk Zine magazine. The anthologies he has edited include *Splatterpunk's Not Dead* (2016), *Splatterpunk Fighting Back* (2017, with Kit Power), *Splatterpunk Forever* (2018, with Kit Power), *Past Indiscretions: The Very Best of Splatterpunk Zine* (2019) and *Splatterpunk Bloodstains* (2020).
Splatterpunk Zine Website: www.splatterpunkzine.wordpress.com

THE DRIVE IN

Author: **Joe R. Lansdale**
Publisher: Bantam Spectra
Year of Publication: 1988
Genre: Horror
Splatterpunk / Bizzarro
Typology: Novel
Total Score: 92
Goodreads Score: 3,91

This short splatterpunk novel is the first chapter of *The Drive-In* trilogy. The author begins by taking us to a huge Texan drive-in cinema full of people. On the screen, the Friday All-Night Horror Show plays: a marathon of B-movies full of monsters and gratuitous gore. Four friends are ready to enjoy the fun—but the on-screen terror merges into reality, turning the drive-in itself into a horror film. The viewers all find themselves trapped by a strange force which materializes like ink and envelops the place. With the crowd now forced to survive only on the available resources, bedlam ensues: inciting cannibalism, rape, murder and crucifixion, showing us the worst, anarchic and primordial face of human nature. This must-read splatterpunk black comedy anticipated the bizarro subgenre.

THE END OF THE END OF EVERYTHING

Author: **Dale Bailey**
Publisher: Arche Press
Year of Publication: 2015
Genre: Weird / Dark Fantasy / Dark SciFi
Typology: Story Collection
Total Score: 88
Goodreads Score: 4,24

A fresh and suggestive collection, this author's vision of horror is mediated by literary-style prose that guides us into the depths of the human condition. But there is no lack of humor here, either. A harmonious fusion of horror and dark fantasy (and dark SciFi) is used to interpret heterogeneous themes, often with an apocalyptic background. Yes, many of these stories concern the end of the world—either by a clear common thread, or a more nuanced undertone. Among my favorite stories include *The Bluehole*, *Mating Habits of the Late Cretaceous*, *A Rumor Of Angels*, *Lightning Jack's Last Ride*, *The Creature Recants* and *The End of the End of Everything*. A book recommended for everyone—except perhaps those looking for more classically-styled horror.

THE FERRYMAN

Author: **Christopher Golden**
Publisher: Signet
Year of Publication: 2002
Genre: Horror / Dark Fantasy
Typology: Novel
Total Score: 84
Goodreads Score: 3,55

An interesting retelling of the myth of Charon, the ferryman of the infernal Styx. In this story (which reads like a surreal nightmare), the psychopomp par excellence—revised by the author—falls in love with a human woman, Janine. Janine has just lost a child in birth, and her concurrent near-death experience brings her to the riverbanks as a passenger to be transported to Hades. But the woman refuses to die—throwing the famous silver coins (payment for the passage to the other shore) into the water, thereby managing to stay in the land of the living. But it wasn't just a bad dream—Charon, obsessed, will certainly not give up. He wants Janine back, and the story will involve other characters (and entities) all animating the suspense. The horror is pitched in a subtle, disturbing, subversive way. Here the action is not with the protagonist of the events, but in the author's reinterpretation of ancient mythology and the theme of impossible love. The seamless intertwining and excellent rendering of atmospheres and settings make this book an intriguing read.

THE FINAL RECONCILIATION

Author: **Todd Keisling**
Publisher: Crystal Lake Publishing
Year of Publication: 2017
Genre: Horror
Typology: Novel
Total Score: 88
Goodreads Score 4,26

Thirty years ago a teenage band called The Yellow Kings began recording their first (and last) heavy metal album titled *The Final Reconciliation*—but a tragic accident (incurring nearly 200 deaths) occurred during the opening concert, forever changing the course of their intended future. The only survivor of the group, guitarist Aidan Cross (who never revealed what really happened), finally grants an exclusive interview to clarify the events of that fateful night. The novel is inspired by Chambers' famous Gothic masterpiece *The King in Yellow*, which takes its title from a forbidden theatrical work that drives those who watch it to madness (the work which inspired Lovecraft's equally well-known *Necronomicon*). But in this case it's the songs on an album which spark the maelstrom, opening a portal to another world. A cosmic horror novel (also a coming-of-age story), with some tributes to Lovecraft, Keisling's vivid characters keep the the reader deeply engaged from start to end.

THE FISHERMAN

Author: **John Langan**
Publisher: Word Horde
Year of Publication: 2016
Genre: Horror / Weird
Typology: Novel
Total Score: 93
Goodreads Score: 3,96

Abe has recently lost his wife to cancer, and develops a passion for fishing to calm his soul. Soon he forms a strong bond with his new friend Dan, who—like him—has lived the experience of grief, having lost his own wife and children in an accident. When they go fishing along a secluded stream in New York State, known as Dutchman's Creek, they learn an old story (dating back to the early 20th century) that could remedy their losses. Here they discover dark pacts and secrets, supernatural events, and a mysterious figure named Der Fischer. The two will face a difficult choice if they wish to regain what they have lost. After all, everything has a price. This weird/cosmic horror-inspired novel is masterfully written, interpreting human frailty, redemption and folklore through one of the best minds of fantastic fiction. Recommended for all.

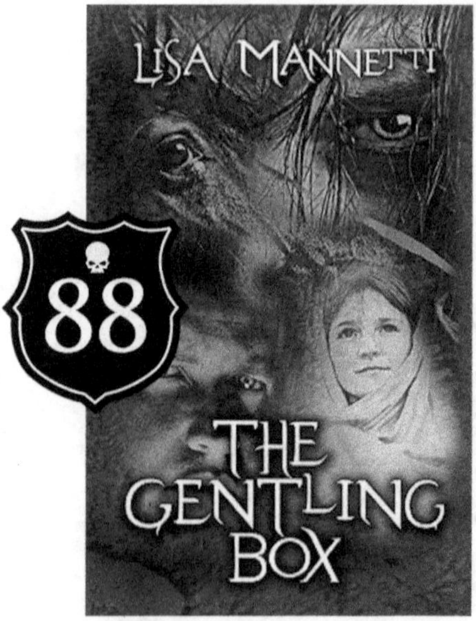

THE GENTLING BOX

Author: **Lisa Mannetti**
Publisher: Dark Hart Press
Year of Publication: 2008
Genre: Horror
Typology: Novel
Total Score: 88
Goodreads Score: 3,74

1865, between Romania and Bulgaria. Imre and his wife Mimi, together with their daughter Lenore and their gypsy community, experience a journey into horror. Between macabre superstitions, sadistic and bloodthirsty magical rites and diabolical possessions, everyone is trapped within a timeless nightmare. The only apparent salvation may be contained within the 'gentling box'—a diabolical device used to tame horses via a subtle torture capable of clearing the mind and freeing it from wicked spirits: in this case the witch Anyeta, devourer of existences. Mannetti's refined prose is well set in this original story of possession with historical roots. There is no lack of brutal scenes here, intimately conveying the unsettling folklore of gypsy culture.

BEST 10 HORROR BOOKS
SELECTED BY

JOE R. LANSDALE

DRACULA by BRAM STOKER (1897)
THE HAUNTING OF HILL HOUSE by SHIRLEY JACKSON (1959)
THE SHINING by STEPHEN KING (1977)
SALEM'S LOT by STEPHEN KING (1975)
THE HOUSE NEXT DOOR by ANN RIVER SIDDONS (1978)
GHOST STORY by PETER STRAUB (1979)
THE SILENCE OF THE LAMBS by THOMAS HARRIS (1988)
A HEAD FULL OF GHOSTS by PAUL TREMBLAY (2015)
THE EXORCIST by WILLIAM PETER BLATTY (1971)
THE ONLY GOOD INDIANS by STEPHEN GRAHAM JONES (2020)

JOE R. LANSDALE is a multiple award-winning American writer. His horror works include *Dead in the West* (1986), *The Nightrunners* (1987) and *The Drive-In* (1988). Website: www.joelansdale.com

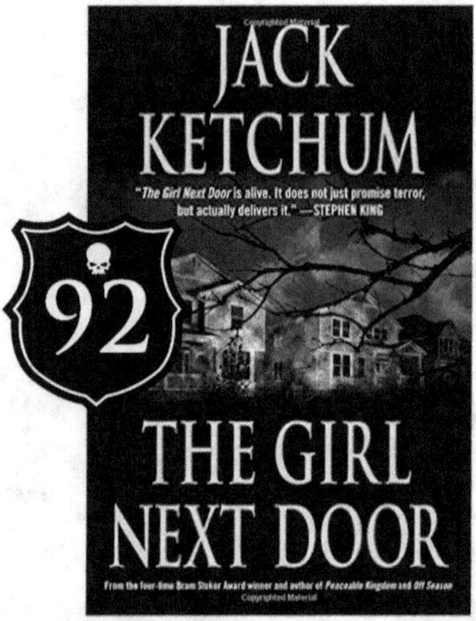

THE GIRL NEXT DOOR

Author: **Jack Ketchum**
Publisher: Leisure
Year of Publication: 1989
Genre: Horror / Thriller
Typology: Novel
Total Score: 92
Goodreads Score: 3,85

One of the best-known works of this great master of horror fiction, who in this book offers us a fictionalized account of a true story: the murder of 16-year-old Sylvia Likens, tortured to death by Gertrude Baniszewski, her children and the young people of their neighborhood in 1965. Here Ketchum forces us to witness what happens in the dark basement of the Chandler house, where Meg and her sister Susan have become prisoners. The sadistic woman also drags her children (and other local kids) into her crimes, and the heinous torture and abuse Meg is subjected to will leave the reader deeply upset. The author's brutal and limpid prose vividly captures themes of insanity and the abuse of children and young people (and the damage of being not only a victim, but also one compliant with such abuse). Not recommended for those who struggle with graphic content.

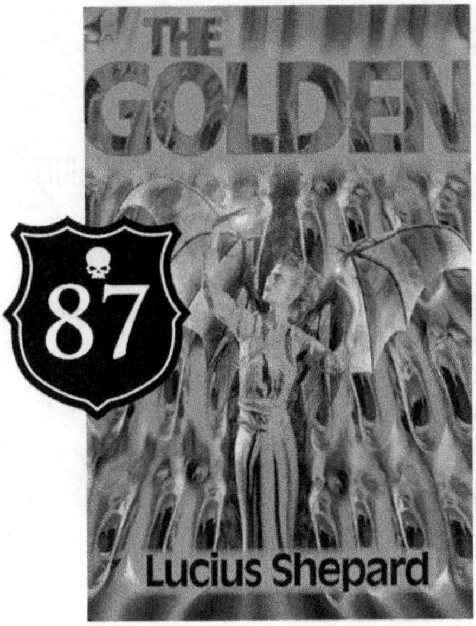

THE GOLDEN

Author: **Lucius Shepard**
Publisher: Golden Gryphon
Year of Publication: 1993
Genre: Horror / Thriller
Typology: Novel
Total Score: 87
Goodreads Score: 3,45

With this novel we are once again among vampire friends. Written with a literary style of the nineteenth century and set in 1860, here Shepard describes the result of the centuries-old experiments that have finally produced 'The Golden': a mortal with perfect blood (in this case, a young girl). Upon hearing the news, various aristocratic clans of vampires gather at Banat Castle to taste the 'sublime blood'. But they discover that the girl has been brutally murdered, and her precious blood already drained. The story then follows the steps of Inspector Beheim (also a vampire) as he works to trace the killer. Between horror and historical settings, dark cults and black ceremonies, multi-dimensions and detective crime, Shepard—a writer of excellence with remarkable prose—puts together a sophisticated, sensual and at times excessive literary novel. A book for fans of the vampire subgenre who appreciate something different.

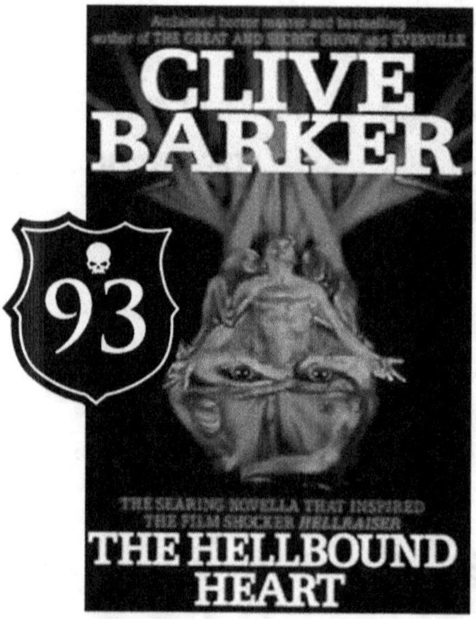

THE HELLBOUND HEART

Author: **Clive Barker**
Publisher: Harper Torch
Year of Publication: 1986
Genre: Horror
Typology: Novella
Total Score: 94
Goodreads Score 4,05

Together with the *Books of Blood*—the best horror work from this great author—this tale introduces the iconic character of Pinhead for the first time. Frank Cotton's insatiable appetite for the most extreme pleasures has led him to solve the puzzle of the Lemarchand box: a portal capable of granting access to an extra-dimensional world inhabited by the Cenobites. These demons are devoted to unfathomable and extreme carnal pleasures, and they imprison him in a limbo state of eternal torture and suffering. But his brother's wife, Julia, has found a way to bring Frank back to life and free him from his prison of pain—even at a terrible price. An innovative work written with high level prose, Barker's formidable prowess with imagery is on full display, and marks the first BDSM inclusions in modern horror fiction. The well-known movie *Hellraiser* (1987), directed by Barker himself, was based on this novella.

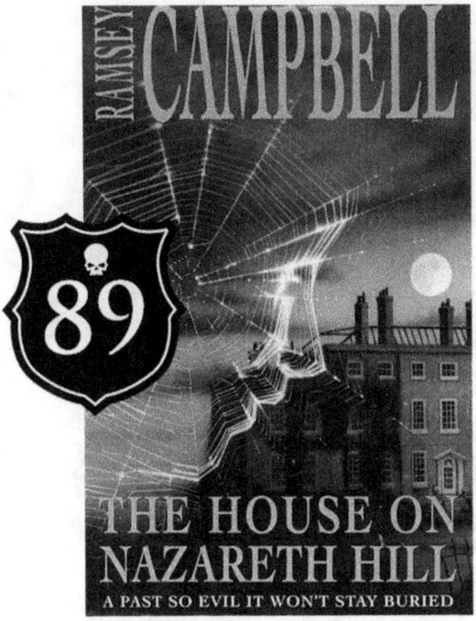

THE HOUSE ON NAZARETH HILL

Author: **Ramsey Campbell**
Publisher: Tom Doherty Association LLC
Year of Publication: 1996
Genre: Horror
Typology: Novel
Total Score: 89
Goodreads Score: 3,5

Campbell's inspired interpretation of the 'haunted place' trope. Widower Oswald Priestley and his teenage daughter Amy move into a renovated mansion. Since she was a child, Amy has always called this place—abandoned for decades—'the house of spiders'. None of the tenants of the new, luxurious building know that Nazareth Hill was once a home to pain and torture. Relations between father and daughter become increasingly difficult. Oswald seems to be affected by the evil essence of the house and its ghostly past, while Amy finds herself facing terrifying visions as she uncovers disturbing secrets. The author, through his disturbing literary prose, dwells on the border between real and supernatural, nightmare and madness, giving life to a dramatic story with a family background, opening ancestral fears. The old horrors of Nazareth Hill are just waiting to re-emerge in full force. Highly enjoyable, this is a book for everyone.

THE HUNGER

Author: **Alma Katsu**
Publisher: G.P. Putnam's Sons
Year of Publication: 2018
Genre: Horror
Typology: Novel
Total Score: 84
Goodreads Score: 3,65

This novel is inspired by the epic 'Donner Expedition', the true story of a group of American pioneers who left for California in a column of wagons and were forced to spend the winter of 1846-7 camped in the Sierra Nevada. Stranded with scarce reserves, some famously resorted to cannibalism to survive, feeding on the dead. Katsu adds supernatural tints to the story with the character of Tamsen Donner, suspected of witchcraft, to explain the misfortunes faced by the expedition. Some pioneers disappear, and the party believe themselves victims of something disturbing hidden in the mountains. There are several enemies to face in order to survive: the inhospitable environment, the severe testing of the human soul, and something mysterious, primitive and ferocious. Katsu is skilled at writing historical horror, recalling Dan Simmons' novel *The Terror*. Recommended for everyone.

THE JIGSAW MAN

Author: **Gord Rollo**
Publisher: EnemyOne
Year of Publication: 2006
Genre: Horror
Typology: Novel
Total Score: 87
Goodreads Score: 3,81

A modern reinterpretation of Mary Shelley's classic *Frankenstein*. Michael Fox is homeless and lives in a dumpster under the Carver Street Bridge in Buffalo. His life is miserable, and he's thinking of getting it over with—but then something unexpected changes the game. A mysterious billionaire surgeon, Dr Marshall, offers him two million dollars to remove his right arm. However, this is just the beginning. By the end, Michael's body will be stripped of many other pieces, only to be reassembled with parts from several other 'donors'. Is Michael still a man, or is he a monster? He doesn't know anymore. The only thing he's sure about is his desire to take revenge on the one who turned him into The Jigsaw Man. The author's first person prose is streamlined and engaging; in my opinion this is the best book by this brilliant horror fiction artist.

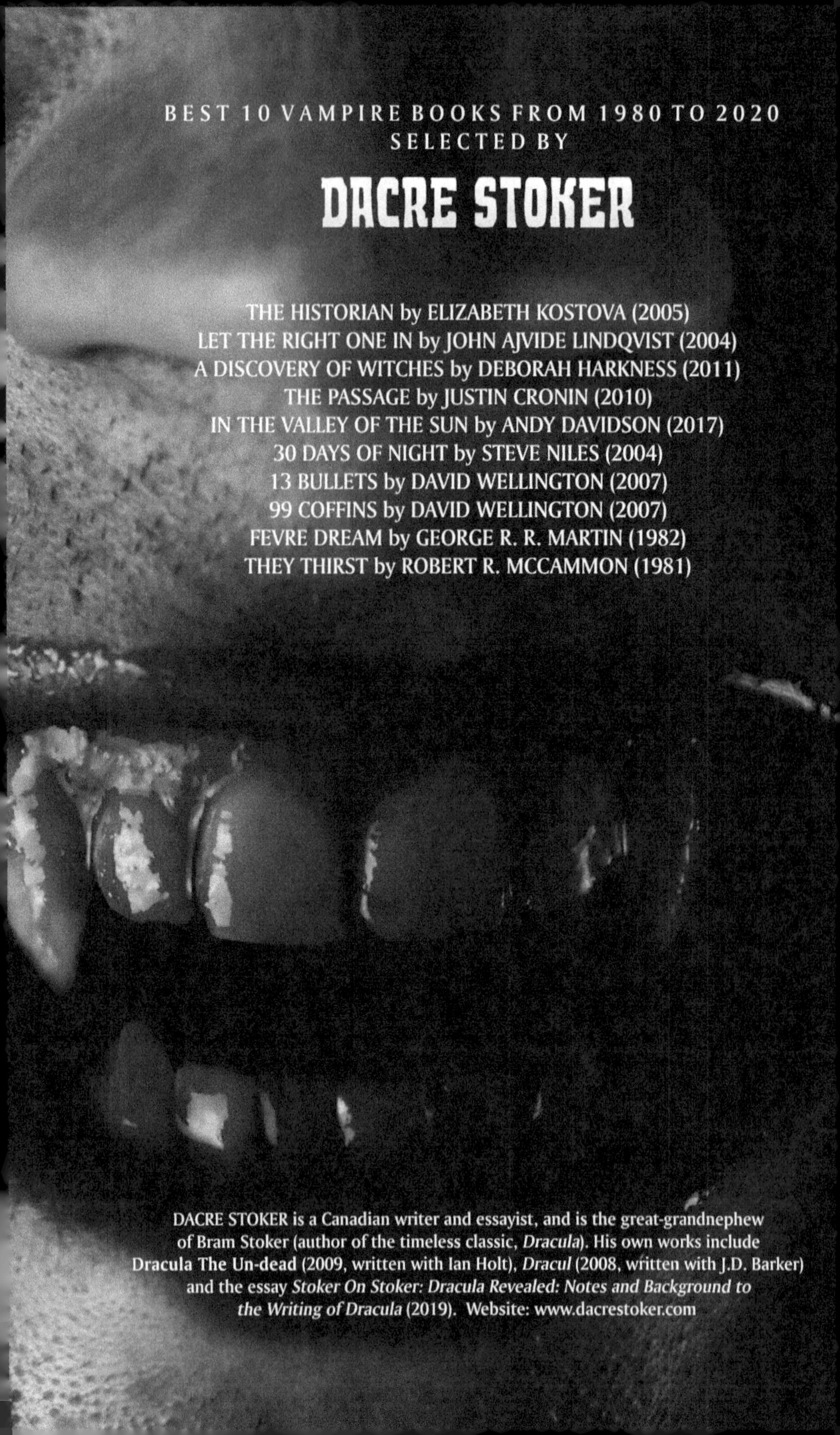
BEST 10 VAMPIRE BOOKS FROM 1980 TO 2020
SELECTED BY
DACRE STOKER
THE HISTORIAN by ELIZABETH KOSTOVA (2005)
LET THE RIGHT ONE IN by JOHN AJVIDE LINDQVIST (2004)
A DISCOVERY OF WITCHES by DEBORAH HARKNESS (2011)
THE PASSAGE by JUSTIN CRONIN (2010)
IN THE VALLEY OF THE SUN by ANDY DAVIDSON (2017)
30 DAYS OF NIGHT by STEVE NILES (2004)
13 BULLETS by DAVID WELLINGTON (2007)
99 COFFINS by DAVID WELLINGTON (2007)
FEVRE DREAM by GEORGE R. R. MARTIN (1982)
THEY THIRST by ROBERT R. MCCAMMON (1981)
DACRE STOKER is a Canadian writer and essayist, and is the great-grandnephew of Bram Stoker (author of the timeless classic, *Dracula*). His own works include Dracula The Un-dead (2009, written with Ian Holt), *Dracul* (2008, written with J.D. Barker) and the essay *Stoker On Stoker: Dracula Revealed: Notes and Background to the Writing of Dracula* (2019). Website: www.dacrestoker.com

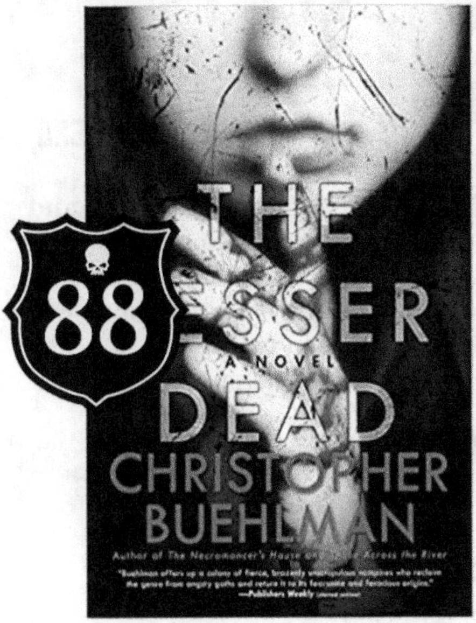

THE LESSER DEAD

Author: **Christopher Buehlman**
Publisher: Berkley
Year of Publication: 2014
Genre: Horror
Typology: Novel
Total Score: 88
Goodreads Score: 4,00

New York, 1978, Joey Peacock is a 14-year-old vampire (in appearance) who has lived the last 60 years as a vampire, and here he tells us his story. The night is obviously the time of the hunt, and Joey feeds in discos, homes and especially on the subway: his favorite larder. He prefers women, favouring their femoral arteries. All is easy, repetitive and satisfying—but one day he see something inside a subway tunnel that changes everything: the ‘happy-eyed children’ which may or may not be vampires like him. Visceral and incisive with intense prose, this book goes beyond the usual vampire clichés. There’s a plenty of blood here, especially in the last brutal section. Recommended for fans of vampire tales.

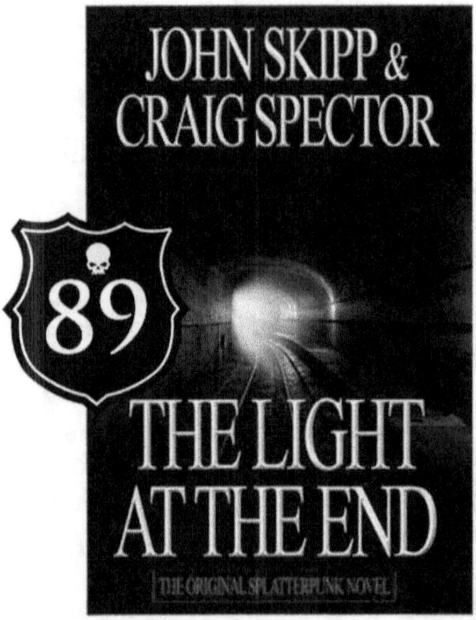

THE LIGHT AT THE END

Author: **John Skipp and Craig Spector**
Publisher: Stealth Press
Year of Publication: 1986
Genre: Horror / Splatterpunk
Typology: Novel
Total Score: 89
Goodreads Score: 3,83

The original cult book of the splatterpunk subgenre, and the debut of this award-winning duo. Given the alphabetical order of book titles in this guide, this entry follows the novel by Buehlman. Here, too, we find vampires on the subway—but this novel was written almost thirty years earlier, at the beginning of the golden age of splatterpunk. The story details a series of murders in the New York subway in the late 1980s, which leave the police at a total loss. The unstoppable killer, who arouses mass hysteria in the city, is described as a demon and is dubbed the 'Subway Psycho'. The villain, Rudy Pasko, represents humanity's most ancient and ruthless evil, and is an unforgettable character. With adrenaline-pumping storytelling and violent content set to a bloody rhythm, this pioneering book is a must-read for fans of the genre.

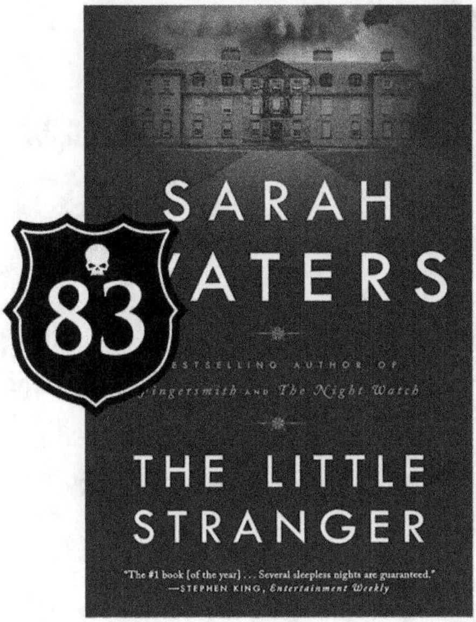

THE LITTLE STRANGER

Author: **Sarah Waters**
Publisher: Riverhead Books
Year of Publication: 2009
Genre: Horror / Mystery
Typology: Novel
Total Score: 83
Goodreads Score: 3,56

In a post-World War II summer, Dr Faraday is called by a patient to the dilapidated Georgian Hundreds Hall, Warwickshire, which has belonged to the aristocratic Ayres family for two centuries and now stands in ruins. As a child thirty years earlier, the doctor was always fascinated by the splendor of this house. But now everything has changed, and the decline of the place is disturbing and ghostly. What feeds the unhealthy virus that seems to envelop everything? Is it the sick psyche of the fallen family surrounded by a world now changed, or is it a mysterious supernatural presence? Everyone thinks that the cause of the strange events now occurring in the house must be some sort of haunting, but Dr Faraday cannot convince himself of this. This Welsh author knows how to evoke the right atmosphere and fill it with suspense, and she skillfully deals with the social dynamics of the time. A book with a very 'British' spirit, this one will appeal to readers fascinated by mysterious old places.

THE MAN ON THE CEILING

Author: **Steve Rasnic Tem and Melanie Tem**
Publisher: Wizards of the Coast Discoveries
Year of Publication: 2008
Genre: Dark Fantasy
Typology: Novel
Total Score: 90
Goodreads Score: 3,47

An original family portrait is displayed in this collaborative work derived from an award-winning short story which straddles narrative (with dark fantasy elements) and memoir, reinforced by the usual surrealism that characterizes the authors' writing. It isn't easy to categorize this work, made up as it is of different pictures (like portraits), each of which allows the reader to peek into the history of a family. The theme, alternating between the two authors in the form of flashbacks, deals with children and parental experience, and the consequent archetypal fears and feelings of guilt. The plot becomes invisible, blurred. Based on the adoption of five children (with their previous experiences and relationships now established in a new environment) there is darkness and nightmares, but also love, acceptance and perseverance. There are no monsters, ghosts or blood here. This is a literary and creative interpretation (which also itself embraces the art of writing) that touches the dark fantasy genre. A book not for everyone, especially readers who prefer their horror with a harsher flavor.

THE MEMORY TREE

Author: **John R. Little**
Publisher: Nocturne Press
Year of Publication: 2007
Genre: Horror / Mystery
Typology: Novel
Total Score: 86
Goodreads Score 4,25

This work posits the idea of going back in one's life to change the past, especially if it hides deep scars. But this is not just about time travel (or alternate realities), this story also details the problem of accuracy—or lack thereof—in memories, and how we adapt them into our existing realities. Sam Elis, a middle-aged stockbroker, finds another self (from the summer of 1968, when he was 13) with whom he can interact. We discover a nightmare life marred by abusive alcoholic parents and sexual abuse by relatives. Over this particularly destructive summer, Sam's brother dies in Vietnam and his best friend is killed. As the author himself says, the past never dies. Rich in subplots, this fascinating and sharp psychological horror and mystery book is captivating and touching. Written with a lucid prose, this book is recommended for everyone.

THE MOUTH OF THE DARK

Author: **Tim Waggoner**
Publisher: Flame Tree Press
Year of Publication: 2018
Genre: Horror / Dark Fantasy
Typology: Novel
Total Score: 84
Goodreads Score: 3,84

A 20-year-old girl has disappeared, and her father, Jayce, believes she has ended up in 'Shadow'—a dark dimension parallel to ours where nightmares become reality. He'll do anything to find her, facing down whatever that bizarre world puts before him: weird fantastic creatures, mad killers, dog eaters, lethal and evil sex toys, psychotic hunters, and a monster called 'Harvest Man'. In this hellish, creepy journey flanked by the darker aspects of sex, the author utilises his usual skill to outline all the surreal and disturbing details, many of which are brutal, showcasing explicit content not suitable for everyone.

BEST 10 HORROR BOOKS FROM 1986 TO 2020
BY BLACK WRITERS SELECTED BY

LINDA D. ADDISON

BELOVED by TONY MORRISON (1987)
MY SOUL TO KEEP by TANANARIVE DUE (1997)
BROWN GIRL IN THE RING by NALO HOPKINSON (1998)
FLEDGLING by OCTAVIA E. BUTLER (2005)
THE GILDA STORIES by JEWELLE L. GÓMEZ (1991)
LET'S PLAY WHITE by CHESYA BURKE (2011)
THE DEVIL IN SILVER by VICTOR LAVALLE (2012)
WHITE IS FOR WITCHING by HELEN OYEYEMI (2009)
WHO FEARS DEATH by NNEDI OKORAFOR (2010)
NINE BAR BLUES by SHEREE RENÉE THOMAS (2020)

LINDA D. ADDISON is an award-winning American writer and poet, and is the first African American author to have won the Bram Stoker Award. Her works include *Animated Objects* (1997), *Consumed, Reduced to Beautiful Gray Ashes* (2001), *Being Full of Light, Insubstantial* (2007), How to Recognize a Demon Has Become Your Friend (2011) and *The Place of Broken Things* (2019, written with Alessandro Manzetti). She edited the short story anthology by African American authors *Sycorax's Daughters* (2017).

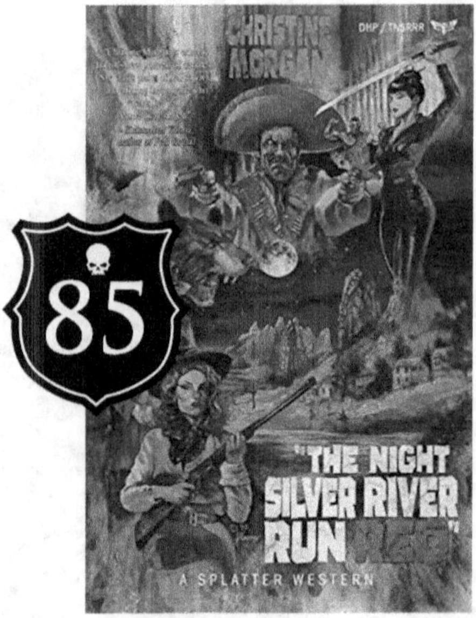

THE NIGHT SILVER RIVER RUN RED

Author: **Christine Morgan**
Publisher: Death's Head Press
Year of Publication: 2020
Genre: Horror / Splatterpunk
Typology: Novel
Total Score: 85
Goodreads Score: 4,15

An explosive, gory and fun splatterpunk/western coming-of-age novel. The protagonist is Cody McCall, a little boy who lives in the quiet town of Silver River. Always looking for something new and stimulating with his friends, an exciting opportunity soon arrives and the group of young people sneaks away to watch an exotic traveling show in the suburbs. Everyone is talking about the magical and grotesque attractions promised at the dark carnival—but other people will also converge in that place, and not with such good intentions. The premise is in some ways reminiscent of Laymon's *Traveling Vampire Show*, but the spirit of this book is completely different. The content is graphic (we are talking about new splatterpunk) but does not fill the whole work, inserted by the author only when needed. The (high-paced) prose and dialogue are brilliant, and the characters are wild and extravagant. Recommended for fans of this specific genre.

THE NIGHTRUNNERS

Author: **Joe R. Lansdale**
Publisher: Carroll & Graf
Year of Publication: 1987
Genre: Horror / Thriller
Typology: Novel
Total Score: 87
Goodreads Score: 3,77

A brutal and dark offering from one of the most brilliant minds in the genre. In this book, Lansdale seats us in a black '66 Chevy and transports us to a hunting story set in Galveston, Texas, in the mid '80s. The main characters are Becky and Montgomery Jones, who are both tormented by recent traumas and are trying to take back their lives. The hunters, on the other hand, are a band of devilish and stoned teenagers. Their new leader, Brian, believes himself possessed by an evil entity (the God of the Razor). This violent, brutal and graphic work is full of suspense, mercilessly revealing the dark and twisted side of the human soul through a piece of modern America. In the end the reader is left feeling dirty for everything he's been through. Given the violent content, this one is not for everyone.

THE ONES THAT GOT AWAY

Author: **Stephen Graham Jones**
Publisher: Prime Books
Year of Publication: 2010
Genre: Horror
Typology: Story Collection
Total Score: 88
Goodreads Score: 3,86

This collection of 13 stories drags us into the darkness before lighting a fuse of bizarre and supernatural elements set in everyday life, leading us to reflect on the humanity of the characters. A father and son are lost in the wilderness, and eat a miraculous, regenerating rabbit to survive. A man and a woman are trapped on an island. A detective who is about to retire faces his final case. A group of marginalized boys throws a supposed witch into the lake. Here we find vampires, bogeymen and urban legends. The author's prose—with his natural, non-conformist style and smooth rhythm—is evocative and visceral, excellently balanced between direct-drive horror and its literary forms. With surprises always found around the corner, this book is recommended for everyone. My favorite stories include *Raphael*, *Monsters*, *So Perfect*, *Captain's Lament* and *Crawlspace*.

THE ONLY GOOD INDIANS

Author: **Stephen Graham Jones**
Publisher: Gallery/Saga Press
Year of Publication: 2020
Genre: Horror
Typology: Novel
Total Score: 92
Goodreads Score: 3,76

Another book by Graham Jones, this novel uses the stories of four childhood friends (Lewis, Ricky, Gabe and Cass) to offer a vivid portrait of the identity of Native Americans. It's the last day of moose hunting season, and the friends do something wrong—they enter a territory reserved for the elders of their tribe, where a supernatural entity (a female spirit with a moose head) will seek to take revenge on them. Now the hunters become the prey. This truly original author's great storytelling skills animate brutal and terrifying moments with prose that balances between the traditional and the avant-garde. The sub-themes here include those close to him (the intergenerational trauma of Native Americans) and the more general, such as hope, family ties, and the horror of injustice and separation from traditions. Stephen Graham Jones is a Blackfeet Native American, a people of the great North American plains to which the protagonists of the novel belong.

BEST 10 HORROR STORIES FROM 1986 TO 2020
SELECTED BY

MORT CASTLE

THE BEES by DAN CHAON (2012)
PIN by ROBERT R. MCCAMMON (1990)
ALL THAT YOU LOVE WILL BE CARRIED AWAY by STEPHEN KING (2001)
TATTOO by BONNIE JOE CAMPBELL (2012)
THE CREATURE FROM THE BLACK LAGOON by JIM SHEPARD (2004)
THE TREE MUMBLERS by PETE MESLING (2020)
THE NIGHT THEY MISSED THE HORROR SHOW by JOE R. LANSDALE (2006)
THE BOOK OF WEBSTERS by J. N. WILLIAMSON (1993)
MR. HANDLEBARS by MARK POWERS (2006)
BEST NEW HORROR by JOE HILL (2007)

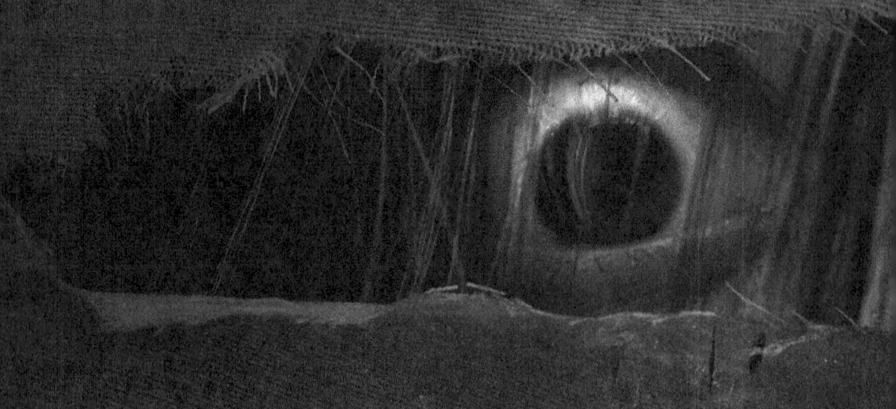

MORT CASTLE is an acclaimed American writer and editor. His works include the novels *The Deadly Election* (1976), *The Strangers* (1984), *Cursed Be the Child* (1990), and the collections *Moons on the Water* (2000) and *Knowing When to Die* (2017). He edited *Shadow Show: All-New Stories in Celebration of Ray Bradbury* (2012, with Sam Weller) and *All-American Horror of the 21st Century: The First Decade: 2000-2010* (2012).

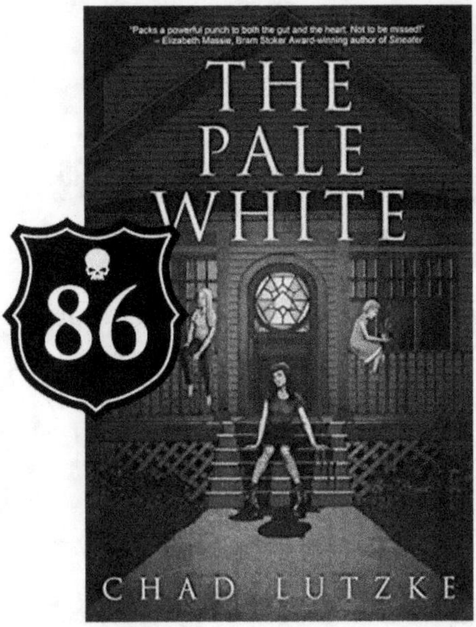

THE PALE WHITE

Author: **Chad Lutzke**
Publisher: Crystal Lake Publishing
Year of Publication: 2019
Genre: Horror / Thriller
Typology: Novella
Total Score: 86
Goodreads Score 4,20

Three young girls (Alex, Stacia and Kammie) are held captive by a certain 'Doc' in the dark attic of a beach house where they are exploited as sex slaves before finally managing to escape. But it will not be easy to face the world that awaits them outside. The signs of what they have suffered are profound, but the horrors of their shared experiences have created a strong relationship between them. The theme of sex trafficking—especially the abuse of young people and children—and the effects on the psychology of the victims are not easy to develop. The author proposes a brutal and disturbing interpretation, channeling this topical subject matter with dignity and respect. Pain, survival, hope and revenge intersect in this very human, brilliantly narrated story (no monsters and spirits here), allowing us into the heads of the protagonists.

THE RAIN DANCERS

Author: **Greg F. Gifune**
Publisher: DarkFuse
Year of Publication: 2012
Genre: Horror / Thriller
Typology: Novella
Total Score: 91
Goodreads Score: 4,04

An intense and touching novella. Will and Betty Colby return to Betty's hometown to fix up her late father's house so they can sell it. The woman's difficult relationship with her father immediately emerges—but then, in the middle of a storm, an unexpected visitor swiftly turns the tone. Bob Laurent, claiming to be an old friend of the family, introduces himself to the couple. Betty doesn't remember him, but the man seems to know everything about her and her missing father. Something is wrong, and suspicion, fear and discomfort take hold in Betty and her husband. They can feel and smell the demons of the past, and it seems clear the stranger has something to claim. Before the storm subsides, the truth will come out. An artfully written, disturbing and deep supernatural psychological thriller that slowly allows all the pieces of a dark mosaic to emerge.

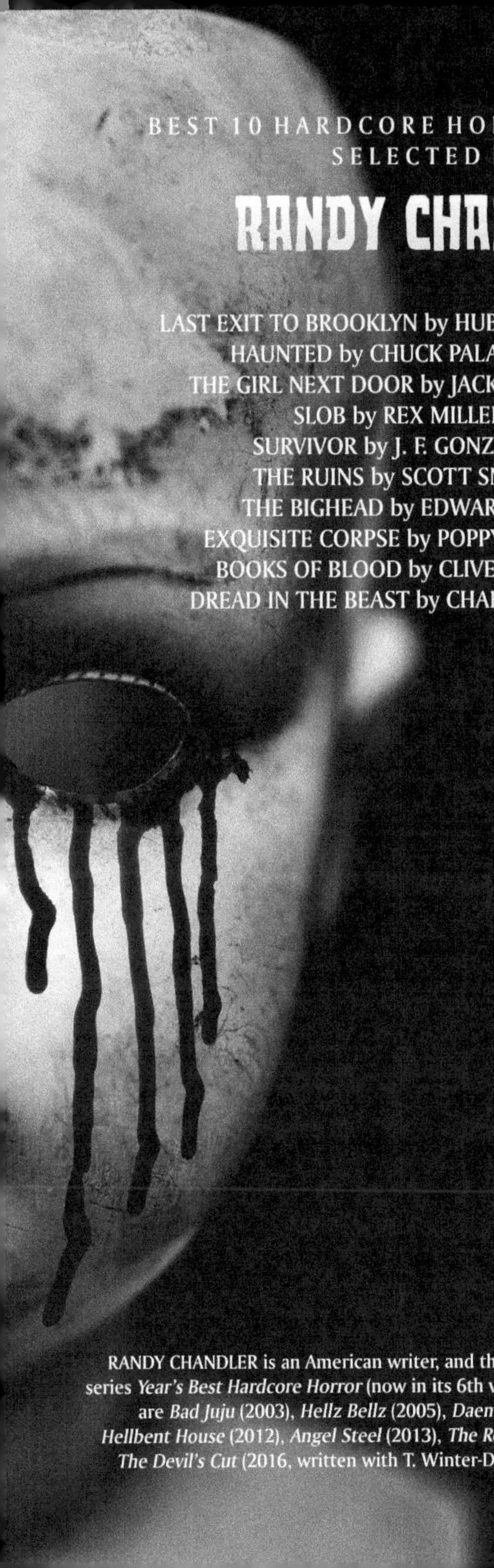

BEST 10 HARDCORE HORROR BOOKS
SELECTED BY

RANDY CHANDLER

LAST EXIT TO BROOKLYN by HUBERT SELBY JR. (1964)
HAUNTED by CHUCK PALAHNIUK (2005)
THE GIRL NEXT DOOR by JACK KETCHUM (1989)
SLOB by REX MILLER (1987)
SURVIVOR by J. F. GONZALEZ (2004)
THE RUINS by SCOTT SMITH (2006)
THE BIGHEAD by EDWARD LEE (1997)
EXQUISITE CORPSE by POPPY Z. BRITE (1996)
BOOKS OF BLOOD by CLIVE BARKER (1984)
DREAD IN THE BEAST by CHARLEE JACOB (1998)

RANDY CHANDLER is an American writer, and the editor of the annual anthology series *Year's Best Hardcore Horror* (now in its 6th volume). Among his works of fiction are *Bad Juju* (2003), *Hellz Bellz* (2005), *Daemon of the Dark Wood* (2012), *Hellbent House* (2012), *Angel Steel* (2013), *The Red Veil* (2014), *Forbidden Gospels: The Devil's Cut* (2016, written with T. Winter-Damon) and *Stolen Roads* (2019).

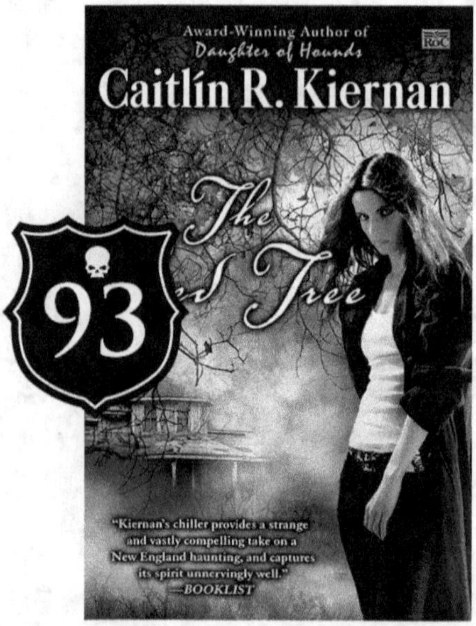

THE RED TREE

Author: **Caitlín R. Kiernan**
Publisher: Ace Books
Year of Publication: 2009
Genre: Horror
Typology: Novel
Total Score: 93
Goodreads Score: 3,67

In Kiernan's fascinating novel, the main character, Sarah (a middle-aged writer), leaves Atlanta following the death of her partner to move to an old Rhode Island country house. Here she discovers a manuscript on local folklore, written by the former tenant—an anthropologist obsessed with the ancient red oak found on the property. The tree, linked to remote and dark legends (human sacrifices, cannibalism and more), will plant its roots in Sarah's imagination, guiding her to transfer her emotions to paper. The story is told in the first person, and Sarah's dreams, merging with reality, begin the disintegration phase of her psyche until she reaches madness. Kiernan, who once again proves herself to be an excellent writer of the fantastic, fills this book with otherworldly sensations, fragile human emotions, and an aching sense of loneliness.

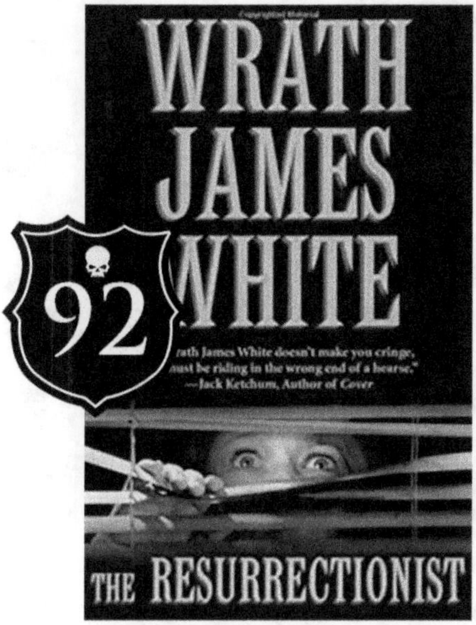

THE RESURRECTIONIST

Author: **Wrath James White**
Publisher: Leisure
Year of Publication: 2009
Genre: Extreme Horror / Splatterpunk
Typology: Novel
Total Score: 92
Goodreads Score: 3,76

The best work, in my opinion, of one of the most important interpreters of new splatterpunk and hardcore/extreme horror. The premise of the book is a striking one. The protagonist, Dale, has the ability to resurrect the dead (provided they are fresh and recently deceased) but, being a sociopath, he has no desire to use this gift for good . . . as a young couple soon experiences firsthand. One can easily imagine the monstrous 'repetitions' done to these victims—the worst atrocities and abuses—without spoiling the story. But in short, Dale is not the best neighbor. The author spares nothing, showing us every possible detail (and then some). A book not for everyone given its brutal and bloody content (violence, torture, rape), this is nevertheless a must for fans of this specific subgenre.

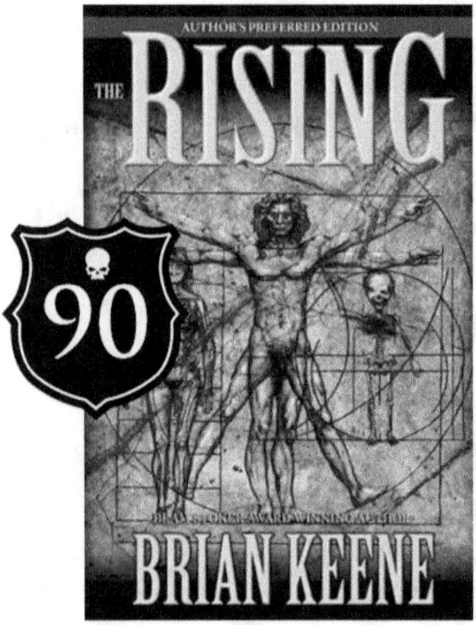

THE RISING

Author: **Brian Keene**
Publisher: Leisure
Year of Publication: 2003
Genre: Horror
Typology: Novel
Total Score: 90
Goodreads Score: 3,79

A novel that, for the originality of the interpretation of the zombie theme, has become a real cult classic. A particle acceleration experiment creates an inter-dimensional rift allowing demons—led by 'Ob'—to possess the bodies of the dead, unleashing a zombie epidemic. The protagonist of the story, Jim Thurmond, survives the initial onslaught and hides in his fallout shelter, trying to reach his son Danny who lives hundreds of miles away. The rescue mission he then embarks upon will take him across the country in the company of an old preacher, an ex-prostitute and a scientist. Keene's zombies (which include animals as well as humans) are not portrayed with the usual clichés; they are intelligent and . . . demon-possessed. For fans of the genre, this delicacy guarantees fun, action, blood and well-defined characters.

THE RITUAL

Author: **Adam Nevill**
Publisher: Pan Publishing
Year of Publication: 2011
Genre: Horror
Typology: Novel
Total Score: 88
Goodreads Score: 3,62

This novel offered its English author greater notoriety thanks to its movie adaptation of the same name (2017, distributed by Netflix). The story follows four old college friends who enter the Scandinavian hinterland for an excursion into its magnificent landscapes. Surrounded by pristine forests, a shortcut leads them to an isolated old house where they find the macabre remains of ancient pagan rites, artifacts and unidentifiable bones. As they soon discover, they themselves have become prey to a beastly creature. Nevill's characters (and the relationships between them) are fully drawn, and the reader is quickly immersed in this disturbing atmosphere. A survival horror for everyone.

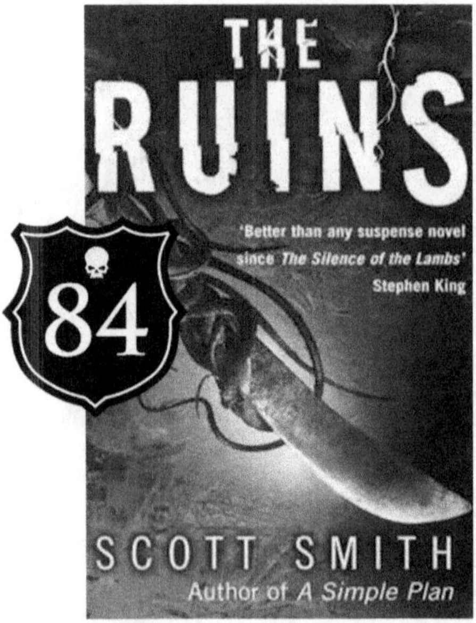

THE RUINS

Author: **Scott Smith**
Publisher: Knopf
Year of Publication: 2006
Genre: Horror / Thriller
Typology: Novel
Total Score: 84
Goodreads Score: 3,60

Defined by Stephen King as the best novel of the new century (a very powerful statement), this fast-paced novel is certainly an enjoyable work. Two couples enjoy a post-graduation vacation in an elegant resort in Cancun. They befriend some other tourists, one of whom convinces them to take a bus and venture with them into the jungle, near a Mayan archaeological dig. The group reaches the ruins, and it is here of course that they find horror (in a different form than the usual). The author is able to fully render the four protagonists (Jeff, Amy, Eric, Stacy) and to animate the suspense. This is another example of high-voltage survival horror. Smith's prose goes straight to the point, without the need for peripheral subtexts and reflections on human nature. Brutal, action-packed and highly engaging, this is a book for everyone.

THE RUST MAIDENS

Author: **Gwendolyn Kiste**
Publisher: Trepidatio Publishing
Year of Publication: 2018
Genre: Horror / Dark Fantasy
Typology: Novel
Total Score: 89
Goodreads Score: 3,75

A dark fantasy (partly coming-of-age), this is the debut novel by one of the most interesting new genre voices. The story is set in Cleveland and told in two different timelines. The main character, Phoebe Shaw, finishes high school with plans to escape Denton Street and her neighborhood, a small town squeezed between the omniscient local steel mill (which is close to collapse) and the abandoned factories that form the backdrop. The first curve of the book reveals that the bodies of five girls from Phoebe's graduation class have been altered by an illness, making them seem to rust and disintegrate (like the neighborhood itself). The girls soon become an attraction for onlookers, tourists, and the government itself. This is a mystery which only the 'Rust Maidens' can explain, and that in itself creates chaos. Kiste's interpretation of the decadence of the American dream, and of social and suburban metamorphoses, makes for fascinating reading. Recommended for everyone, this book is a breath of fresh air in fantastic fiction.

BEST 10 HORROR BOOKS FROM 1986 TO 2020
SELECTED BY

LUCY TAYLOR

THE TERROR by DAN SIMMONS (2007)
THE VISIBLE FILTH by NATHAN BALLINGRUD (2015)
A HEAD FULL OF GHOSTS by PAUL TREMBLAY (2015)
THE CABIN AT THE END OF THE WORLD by PAUL TREMBLAY (2018)
GHOST STORY by PETER STRAUB (1989)
THE HUNGER by ALMA KATSU (2018)
THE DROWNING GIRL by CAITLÍN R. KIERNAN (2012)
THE SILENCE OF THE LAMBS by THOMAS HARRIS (1988)
CARRION COMFORT by DAN SIMMONS (1989)
SWAN SONG by ROBERT R. MCCAMMON (1987)

LUCY TAYLOR is an American writer, and is one of the most important voices in hardcore horror. Among her works include *The Flesh Artist* (1993), *The Safety of Unknown Cities* (1995), *Painted in Blood* (1996), *Sub-Human* (1998), *Eternal Hearts* (1999), Saving Souls (2002), *The Silence Between the Screams* (2004), *Spree and Other Stories* (2018) and *Dancing with Demons* (2019).

THE SAFETY OF UNKNOWN CITIES

Author: **Lucy Taylor**
Publisher: Overlook Connection Press
Year of Publication: 1995
Genre: Horror / Hardcore Horror
Typology: Novel
Total Score: 91
Goodreads Score: 3,67

A novel by one of the most important authors of the hardcore horror subgenre, to which this book also refers. The protagonist, Val, travels from one city and one relationship to another, constantly searching for experiences to fill the void within herself. When she learns of a 'magical' place called City, promising pure and constant pleasure, she is immediately determined to go there. But another obsession enters the story: unbeknownst to her, she is being chased by a psychopathic ex-lover. Taylor's prose is of a high quality, and her explicit content focuses primarily on sex. But here this theme delves much deeper, touching on childhood and lost innocence, referencing the deformation of sexuality in modern society and the complexities of the search for love. This book details a surreal journey, branching off between characters and into parallel realities, and offering an engaging alchemy of horror, sex and suspense.

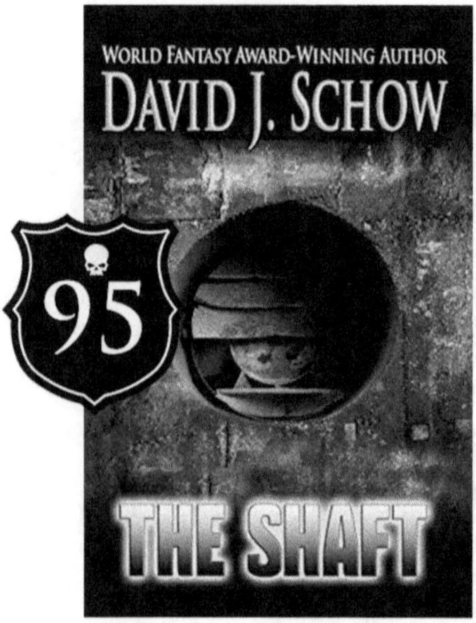

THE SHAFT

Author: **David J. Schow**
Publisher: Futura
Year of Publication: 1990
Genre: Horror / Splatterpunk / Pulp
Typology: Novel
Total Score: 95
Goodreads Score: 3,71

From one of the greatest genre writers, this formidable novel combines the best in the splatterpunk, literary horror and pulp/thriller genres. A petty drug dealer named Cruz finds himself fleeing sunny Miami to take cover in freezing Chicago, where he hides in a rented room in the dilapidated Kenilworth Arms building. Here he meets Jonathan, a yuppie trying to get over a failed romance; and Jamaica, a prostitute in the pay of a drug kingpin known as Bauhaus. When they are forced to throw two kilos of cocaine down a ventilation shaft in a bid to escape a police raid, strange things begin to happen. It is soon discovered that a monstrous creature is hiding in the building . . . at the bottom of that very shaft. Schow's original and refined prose transitions through lyrical, pulp, violent, humorous and surreal storytelling, and his characters are memorable. Nothing is missing here, making this a must-read for all, and not just fans of the genre.

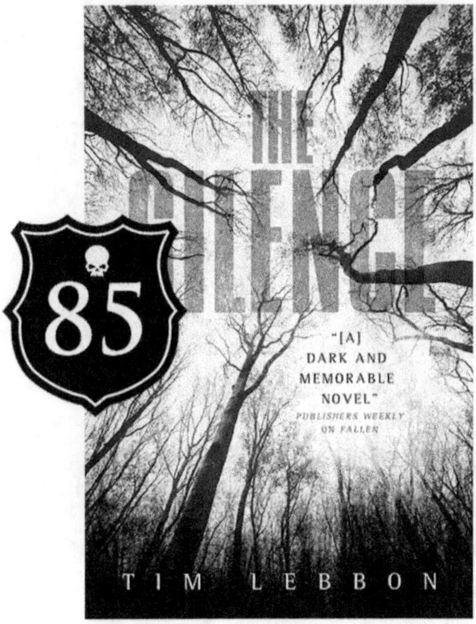

THE SILENCE

Author: **Tim Lebbon**
Publisher: Titan Books
Year of Publication: 2015
Genre: Horror
Typology: Novel
Total Score: 85
Goodreads Score: 3,82

▶ A novel set in the apocalyptic 'sensorial' wake of Malerman's *Bird Box*, this story focuses on human hearing to orchestrate a claustrophobic tale. A group of speleologists unearths an unknown species of deadly pterosaur-like creatures called 'wasps', setting off a fight for survival. Any sound attracts the flying creatures, a new reality we experience through the POV of a family with a small child left deaf due to an accident. The question the author indirectly proposes is: how much would our lives (and our values) change in the face of a radical shift in the dynamics of our living environment? This engaging book is full of suspense, and leaves off with an open ending rather than a fixed conclusion. It has been adapted for the screen, distributed by Netflix.

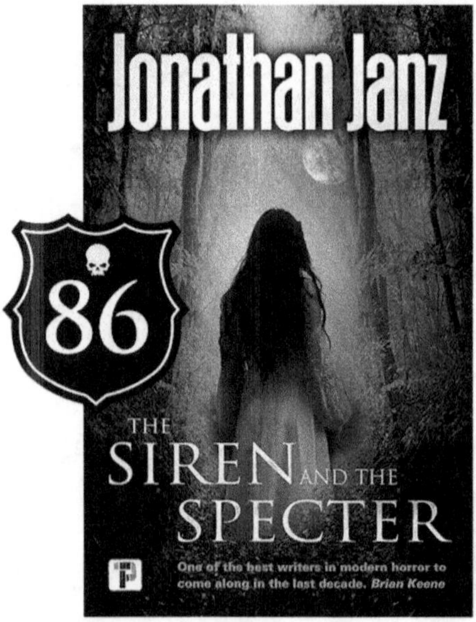

THE SIREN AND THE SPECTER

Author: **Jonathan Janz**
Publisher: Flame Tree Press
Year of Publication: 2018
Genre: Horror
Typology: Novel
Total Score: 86
Goodreads Score: 3,94

With this novel, Janz brings us back to the classic theme of the haunted house. David Caine, a skeptical researcher of the supernatural, is invited by an old friend to spend a month in the most haunted house in Virginia. Caine has already investigated several such houses, and he's expecting another simple case which he can easily debunk. But the Alexander House, built by a baron in the year 1700 for his insane and depraved son Judson—a practitioner of black magic—will prove to be a surprise for the skeptic. In addition to the shadows and mysteries of the Shelby family's past, Caine will discover familiar presences once known to him in his own life. His other finds include the diary of another researcher, one who investigated the house a long time before him. Janz spreads out the fascinating twists, secrets, and revelations (there is also a ghostly island in front of the house) between liberal lashings of fresh blood. A book with a dense atmosphere and skilfully-crafted characters, shrouded in the mists of mystery surrounding the house. Recommended for everyone.

THE SOUTHERN BOOK CLUB'S GUIDE TO SLAYING VAMPIRES

Author: **Grady Hendrix**
Publisher: Quirk Books
Year of Publication: 2020
Genre: Horror / Thriller
Typology: Novel
Total Score: 91
Goodreads Score: 3,82

One of the most interesting genre fiction works of 2020. Patricia Campbell's life after marriage has become unsatisfying: her sons have moved, she's left her job, and she lives unhappily with her husband in a small town that doesn't have much to offer. But luckily, to make her days more interesting, there is the Book Club: a small group of housewives who meet to share their passion for crime and suspense books. Things change when the mysterious and cultured James Harris moves into the neighborhood. Paula, despite the man's strangeness, finds herself attracted to him. But when some black children disappear from the community, she and her friends begin to suspect the newcomer, and they resolve to investigate. Has evil come to Charleston? Their discoveries will bring terrifying results. Hendrix wisely mixes humor and gore, making this book a captivating and entertaining read. Through the Book Club, the author subtly proposes racial and social questions, alluding to the complexities of women and family abuse (physical and psychological), offering us an interesting insight into modern America.

THE TANK

Author: **Nicola Lombardi**
Publisher: Dunwich Edizioni
Year of Publication: 2016
Genre: Horror
Typology: Novel
Total Score: 84
Goodreads Score: 3,97

An intriguing, claustrophobic novel by Italian writer Nicola Lombardi. The premise of this dystopic horror story places us in a future world lead by a military dictatorship establishing the New Moral Order. Here the 'Tanks' offer an extreme detainment system, serving as terrible instruments for a radical purge of society. Giovanni Corte, the main character, attains the desired role of keeper of Tank 9, where he will spend a whole year isolated from the rest of the world, slowly discovering the stark reality of his dehumanized world. Written with depth and detail, this book deals with the themes of conformism and dissension, as well as the oblivion and, obviously, the horror of a totalitarian regime.

THE TERROR

Author: **Dan Simmons**
Publisher: Little, Brown and Company
Year of Publication: 2007
Genre: Horror / Thriller
Typology: Novel
Total Score: 89
Goodreads Score: 4,03

This novel is characterized by its original setting and is inspired by a true story. Simmons' historical fiction account follows the adventures of the Franklin expedition of 1845, as two ships and their crews search for the legendary Northwest Passage. The ships, the Erebus and the Terror, will be trapped by ice for many long months in the Arctic Circle, and the men must survive these extreme conditions. But the real enemy will not be the cold, the hostile environment, the increasingly scarce rations or the desperation that leads to episodes of cannibalism. There is something out there: an invisible and evil predator that hunts the men down, killing them one by one. Here this great author has created a well-detailed, icy nightmare, and the vivid characters (including the Inuit Esquimaux) offer us a clear view into the mindset of Victorian-era sailors, and on the dark mythologies extant at the time concerning unexplored places. Another excellent example of historical genre fiction, this one is highly recommended. The first season of the series of the same name, distributed by Amazon Prime Video, is based on this novel.

BEST 10 HORROR BOOKS FROM 1986 TO 2020
SELECTED BY

KATE JONEZ

THE HUNGER by ALMA KATSU (2018)
THE DROWNING GIRL by CAITLÍN R. KIERNAN (2012)
HEAD FULL OF GHOSTS by PAUL TREMBLAY (2015)
EXPERIMENTAL FILM by GEMMA FILES (2015)
MONGRELS by STEPHEN GRAHAM JONES (2016)
BABY TEETH by ZOJE STAGE (2018)
THE GRIEF HOLE by KAARON WARREN (2016)
THE DEVIL IN SILVER by VICTOR LAVALLE (2012)
THINGS WE LOST IN THE FIRE by MARIANA ENRÍQUEZ (2016)
BIRD BOX by JOSH MALERMAN (2014)

KATE JONEZ, is an American writer and editor, and is the publisher of Omnium Gatherum. Her works of fiction include *Flicker* (2010), *Candy House* (2013), *Ceremonies of Flies* (2014) and *Lady Bits* (2019). She has also edited the anthologies *Detritus* (2012) and *Little Visible Delight* (2013). Website: www.katejonez.com

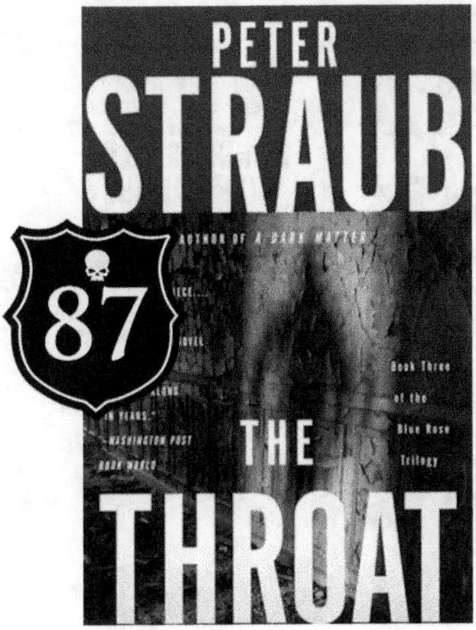

THE THROAT

Author: **Peter Straub**
Publisher: Signet
Year of Publication: 1993
Genre: Horror / Thriller
Typology: Novel
Total Score: 87
Goodreads Score: 3,95

The third novel in the 'Blue Rose' trilogy (after *Koko* and *Mystery*). This instalment can be read independent of the others titles, although some small (largely insignificant) correlations could of course be lost. In this book the author follows the character Tim Underhill, known from the previous novels. Underhill is a writer, and he receives a phone call from an old friend whose wife has been brutally beaten and killed. The attacker has left the words 'Blue Rose' written on a wall at the scene, and this revelation brings Underhill back to the painful events of the past and to the crimes of thirty years ago where the same signature appeared. Underhill returns to his old Midwestern town to track the killer (a copycat?), along with his friend John Ramson and Detective Tom Pasmore. This horror/thriller, with its multi-layered plot, is perhaps the best one of the trilogy. It is without supernatural elements, and is written in dense, descriptive prose. Crime/horror fiction fans will enjoy this book as a sophisticated work that goes beyond mere entertainment.

THE TRAVELING VAMPIRE SHOW

Author: **Richard Laymon**
Publisher: Leisure
Year of Publication: 2000
Genre: Horror
Typology: Novel
Total Score: 93
Goodreads Score: 3,84

In my opinion the best book by Laymon. A fantastic coming-of-age novel, this portrait of adolescence (depicting a world close to the author's heart) is unique among its kind. It's the summer of 1963 in the rural town of Grandville, and flyers have appeared announcing a mysterious evening event: 'The Traveling Vampire Show'. The star of the show is the seductive Valeria, presented as the only vampire in captivity. The main characters are three 16-year-olds: Dwight, Rusty and Slim. Beautifully characterized by Laymon, the trio naturally want to attend the show (at midnight, in an area that is off limits to them), and will have to find a way to get there. This story of friendship captures the dynamics of adolescent relationships, and it's only at the end of the novel that things suddenly turn towards horror. The author only needs a few pages to make us shiver, but the emotions which linger will be those evoked by the vivid sense and memory of youth. A must-read for fans, and indeed for everyone.

THE WORST IS YET TO COME

Author: **S.P. Miskowski**
Publisher: Trepidatio Publishing
Year of Publication: 2019
Genre: Horror
Typology: Novel
Total Score: 85
Goodreads Score: 3,92

A coming-of-age novel set in the rural (and haunted) city of Skillute, Washington, a location already used in the author's other works. Tasha Davis, the teenage protagonist, moves to the town from Seattle and befriends 16-year-old rebel Briar Kenny. Each of them wants something that the other has, coming as they do from very different family backgrounds (two opposing models/archetypes: stability versus dysfunctionality). Following a series of brutal events, their relationship strengthens. But something sinister lurks—a dark force hiding in the town, feeding on their vulnerability and testing the bond between the girls. Moving between past and present, this novel focuses on the relationships between these well-developed characters, adding substance to the fabric and soul of this disturbing existential horror/thriller.

THINGS WE LOST IN THE FIRE

Author: **Mariana Enríquez**
Publisher: Hogarth Press
Year of Publication: 2016
Genre: Horror / Mystery
Typology: Story Collection
Total Score: 90
Goodreads Score: 4,07

A collection of 12 stories by this Argentinian author, exploring the small and large tragedies of the human condition in combination with socio-political themes such as inequality, corruption, drug addiction, military dictatorship and related influences on collective memory. The stories are set in unnamed Argentinian cities and slums, dealing with murders, torture, ghost stories, urban legends, haunted houses, superstitions, nightmares, obsessions, families and disappearances. Among my favorite stories are *Adela's House*, *The Dirty Kid*, *The Neighbor's Courtyard* and *Under the Black Water*. A voice to listen to, deftly projecting us into Argentina with a mastery of rhythm, atmosphere and prose, here we discover how the ghosts of history help create the contemporary world. Recommended for all readers, but the more discerning especially are sure to find something, here.

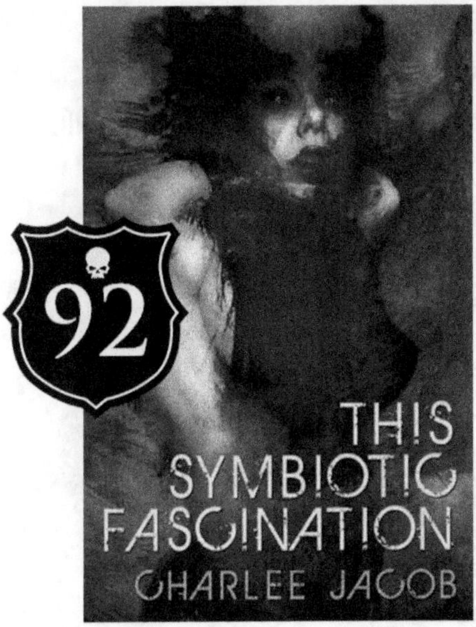

THIS SYMBIOTIC FASCINATION

Author: **Charlee Jacob**
Publisher: Leisure
Year of Publication: 1997
Genre: Hardcore Horror
Typology: Novel
Total Score: 92
Goodreads Score: 3,58

An author who dominates the hardcore horror subgenre, enveloping it in literary, poetic and visionary prose and creating a sparkling dichotomy between surrealist beauty and extreme content. In his debut novel, Jacob (who has since sadly passed away) introduces us to two characters who are both employed in an electronics store: the awkward 37-year-old Tawne Delaney and the misfit Arcan Tyler—who is also a sadistic rapist. The two embody a modern version of the vampire and the werewolf archetypes, and it is through this monstrous pairing (leaving behind them a long trail of blood) that the author portrays affinities with death, exploring the sub-theme of male and female insecurities. This extreme, violent book is full of symbolism and is over the top in every sense, offering the reader a wide, wild array of emotions. This is not for everyone, and I recommend this only for fans of the extreme.

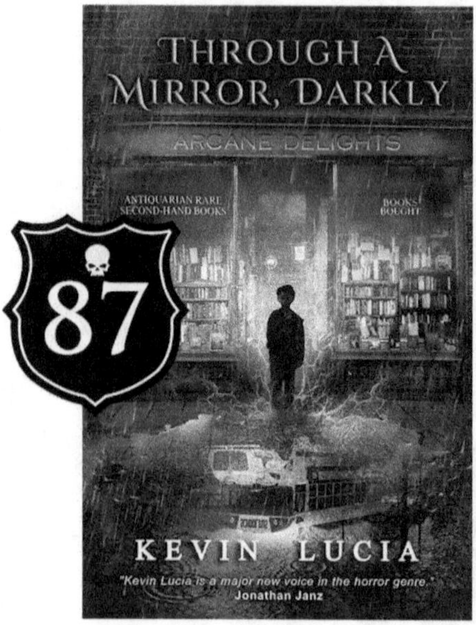

THROUGH A MIRROR, DARKLY

Author: **Kevin Lucia**
Publisher: Crystal Lake Publishing
Year of Publication: 2015
Genre: Horror / Thriller
Typology: Novella Collection
Total Score: 87
Goodreads Score: 4,39

A collection of novellas revolving around a used bookstore called Arcane Delights. The owner, Kevin Ellison, takes possession of a mysterious diary which reveals the dark secrets of his city, the surreal Clifton Heights. This imaginary location has been used by the author in his other works, with the legends and myths of Carcosa always playing an essential role. It's here that these stories unfold in tones of mystery and the supernatural. My favorite novellas include *Yellow Cab* and *And I Watered it, With Tears*. Kevin Lucia, with his lyrical prose and touches of black humor, offers a captivating and subtle interpretation of the genre, offering a new perspective on the everyday thanks to his 'ghost' location, incorporating demons both real and imaginary. Recommended for everyone.

BEST 10 HORROR & DARK POETRY COLLECTIONS FROM 1986 TO 2020 SELECTED BY

LINDA D. ADDISON

THIS CAPE IS RED BECAUSE I'VE BEEN BLEEDING
by TOM PICCIRILLI (2002)
HERESY by CHARLEE JACOB (2006)
THE TROUBLESOME AMPUTEE by JOHN EDWARD LAWSON (2006)
CORONA OBSCURA by MICHAEL R. COLLINGS (2016)
DEMONSTRA by BRYAN THAO WORRA (2013)
DANGEROUS DREAMS by MARGE SIMON & SANDY DELUCA (2013)
SLEEPING UNDER THE TREE OF LIFE
by SHEREE RENÉE THOMAS (2016)
NO MERCY by ALESSANDRO MANZETTI (2017)
DRAGONFLY AND OTHER SONGS OF MOURNING
by MICHELLE SCALISE (2012)
IF YOU DIED TOMORROW I WOULD EAT YOUR CORPSE
by WRATH JAMES WHITE (2018)

LINDA D. ADDISON is an award-winning American writer and poet, and is the first African American author to have won the Bram Stoker Award. Her works include *Animated Objects* (1997), *Consumed, Reduced to Beautiful Gray Ashes* (2001), *Being Full of Light, Insubstantial* (2007), How to Recognize a Demon Has Become Your Friend (2011) and *The Place of Broken Things* (2019, written with Alessandro Manzetti). She edited the short story anthology by African American authors *Sycorax's Daughters* (2017).

UMBRÍA

Author: **Santiago Eximeno**
Publisher: Independent Legions
Year of Publication: 2020
Genre: Horror / Body Horror
Typology: Story Collection
Total Score: 87
Goodreads Score: 4,28

An original collection of nine short stories (including two novelettes) by Nocte Award-winning Spanish author, Santiago Eximeno. Each tale is set in the surreal city of Umbrìa, an underground labyrinth dominated by the mysterious Mister-Red. Umbrìa has its own physical laws and is located outside the normal space-time continuum, constituting a sort of limbo. Anyone overwhelmed by despair, fear or guilt can end up in Umbrìa—entering through a hole in the wall, a strange door, a wardrobe, a mysterious shop—and on arrival instantly lose all memory of their previous life. These ethereal tales depict graphic body horror involving sex, sexual violence, and grotesque, inhuman creatures. In his literary-style prose, Eximeno stages recurring characters and creates something more than a mere collection of short stories. Among the themes developed in this volume are dysfunctional families, relationship problems, alcoholism and domestic abuse, each articulated into the allegorical power of this imaginary city. My favorite stories include *Debris* and *Lambodas*.

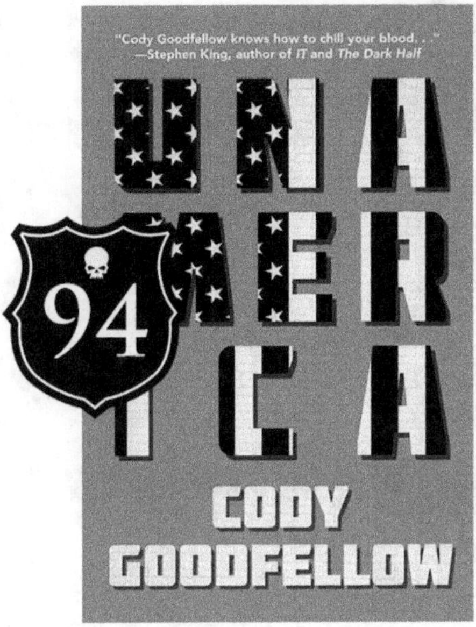

UNAMERICA

Author: **Cody Goodfellow**
Publisher: King Shot Press
Year of Publication: 2019
Genre: Bizzarro / Weird
Typology: Novel
Total Score: 94
Goodreads Score: 4,58

A foray into bizarre dystopian fiction with horror, weird and SciFi elements. Goodfellow is a notable author, and he sets this uncategorizable novel/manifesto in an underground city (named Unamerica) built beneath the desert on the border between the United States and Mexico, where it serves as a sort of government-run social experiment. The main character, Nolan Hatch—who has discovered a drug which makes him capable of communicating (more or less) with God—ends up in this ghetto city. Unamerica is populated by outcasts who have been transformed into human test subjects, and is governed by psychopaths, drug dealers, prophets and criminals who are all at war with each other. Blood and humor run through these pages, captured in the comical and the surreal, coloring the real-world themes Goodfellow so creatively builds upon: capitalism, consumerism, immigration, religion, drug use, inequality, marginalization and much more. A work of political satire somewhere between Burroughs, Dick and Mieville, this work takes the American dream to its extreme limit—and towards mayhem and death.

WHEN THEY CAME BACK

Author: **Christopher Conlon**
Publisher: BearManor Media
Year of Publication: 2013
Genre: Horror
Typology: Novella
Total Score: 89
Goodreads Score: 4,55

Hardgrove, Nebraska, 1899. A small village where nothing important ever happens. A mysterious, oily, skin-scorching substance rains from the sky, marking the beginning of events. After the strange storm, the dead begin to come back to life. Conlon's lyrical and fascinating prose reads like an extravagant, macabre dance, telling us a disturbing and melancholy story as we peer, captivated, into his characters' thoughts. This novella (a highly original interpretation of the zombie trope) differs greatly from the cliché, and shows also the successful collaboration of the author with the photographer Roberta Lannes-Sealey, whose striking black and white works are an integral part of the book, contributing to the atmosphere and sense of estrangement induced by the narrative. Recommended for readers with sophisticated tastes.

BEST 10 HORROR BOOKS FROM 1979 TO 2020
SELECTED BY

CRAIG SPECTOR

SCARS AND OTHER DISTINGUISHING MARKS (Collection) by R.C. MATHESON (1987)
CREATED BY (Novel) by R.C. MATHESON (1993)
BOOKS OF BLOOD (Collection) by CLIVE BARKER (1984/1985)
THE DEAD ZONE (Novel) by STEPHEN KING (1979)
THE SILENCE OF THE LAMBS (Novel) by THOMAS HARRIS (1988)
LOST SOULS (Novel) by POPPY Z. BRITE (1992)
HELL GATE (Novel) by ELIZABETH MASSIE (2013)
SILVER SCREAM (Anthology) Edited by DAVID J. SCHOW (1988)
THE ESSENTIAL ELLISON (Collection) by HARLAN ELLISON (1998)
THE HANDMAID'S TALE (Novel) by MARGARET ATWOOD (1985)

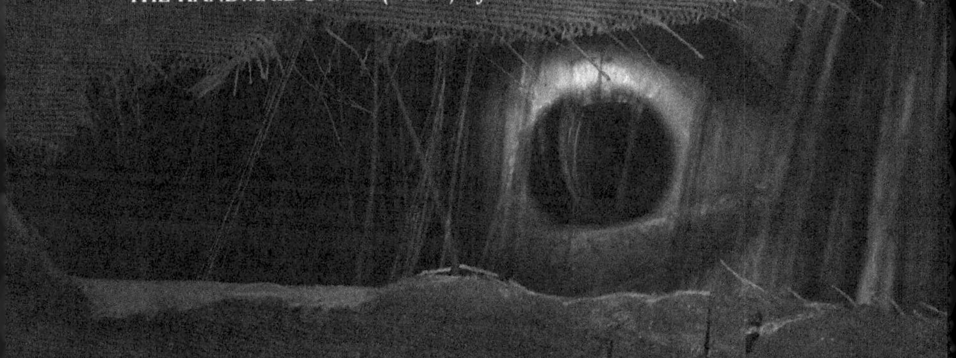

CRAIG SPECTOR is an American writer and editor, and is one of the founders of the Splatterpunk movement. Among his works as an author are the novels *The Light at the End* (1986, written with John Skipp), *The Bridge* (1991, written with John Skipp), *Animals* (1992, written with John Skipp), *To Bury the Dead* (2000), *Underground* (2005), *A Question of Will* (2010) and *Turnaround* (2013).

WHITE TRASH GOTHIC

Author: **Edward Lee**
Publisher: Deadite
Year of Publication: 2017
Genre: Hardcore Horror
Typology: Novel
Total Score: 90
Goodreads Score: 3,99

In this novel, Edward Lee brings together some of his best-known characters in a must-read 'magnum opus' for genre fans, assembling a crazy and wildly entertaining story. The plot follows a writer in the throes of amnesia; in a bid to recover his memory, he returns to his family in the small Appalachian town of Luntville, where he left the first page of a new novel (entitled 'White Trash Gothic'). The town is a jumble of horrors and brutality: a production of extreme films, the ghosts of serial killers, demons, grotesque traditions, necrophilia, depravity of all kinds, and the monstrous The Bighead (the main character of another Lee novel of the same title; while I do recommend reading both that work and *The Minotauress* before this one, it isn't essential). A real hardcore horror funfair with disturbing content, this book is recommended only for fans of this specific subgenre.

WORMWOOD

Author: **Poppy Z. Brite**
Publisher: Dell
Year of Publication: 1993
Genre: Horror
Typology: Story Collection
Total Score: 91
Goodreads Score: 3,91

An inspired collection of short stories from one of the most original and brilliant interpreters of modern dark fiction who, thanks to the lyrical and innovative prose showcased here, marks new boundaries and perspectives for the genre. In this volume you will find some of the author's true classics, such as *His Lips Will Taste of Wormwood*, the famous *Calcutta, Lord of Nerves*, *The Sixth Sentinel*, and *Xenophobia*. From New Orleans, the epicenter of the narrative world of Poppy Z. Brite (now Billy Martin) to a Calcutta invaded by living dead, each tale offers us vivid, borderline, marginalized, libertine characters sucked into a magical and visceral vortex of desires, flesh, sex and death, all resounding with the 'voodoo jazz' of the author's velvety prose.

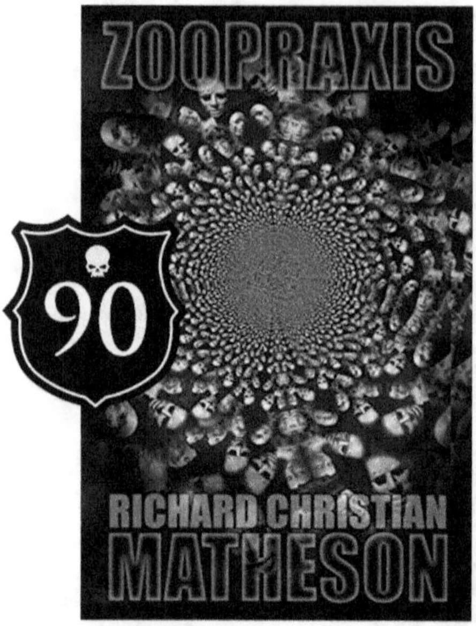

ZOOPRAXIS

Author: **Richard Christian Matheson**
Publisher: Gauntlet Press
Year of Publication: 2016
Genre: Psychological Horror / Magic Realism / Dark Noir
Typology: Story Collection
Total Score: 90
Goodreads Score: 4,44

A collection of short stories by Richard Christian Matheson (son of Richard Matheson, author of the famous *I Am Legend*) ranging from magic realism to dark thriller/noir, this crossing between genres is characterized by a psychological and existential approach. The author's minimalist prose is among the best ever in short fiction, with a hypnotic and evocative tone capable of rousing strong emotions in the reader and stirring striking images. Among my favorite stories are *Transfiguration*, *Talking Man*, *Sea of Atlas* and *Interrogation*.

BEST 10 HORROR BOOKS FROM 1986 TO 2020
SELECTED BY

DAVID G. BARNETT

WEAVEWORLD by CLIVE BARKER (1987)
CONVULSION FACTORY by BRIAN HODGE (1996)
THEY THIRST by ROBERT MCCAMMON (1981)
NECROSCOPE by BRIAN LUMLEY (1986)
CABAL by CLIVE BARKER (1988)
HEADER by EDWARD LEE (1995)
DREAD IN THE BEAST by CHARLEE JACOB (1998)
SHADOWLAND by PETER STRAUB (1980)
PAINFREAK by GERARD HOUARNER (1996)
THE PRESERVE by PATRICK LESTEWKA (2004)

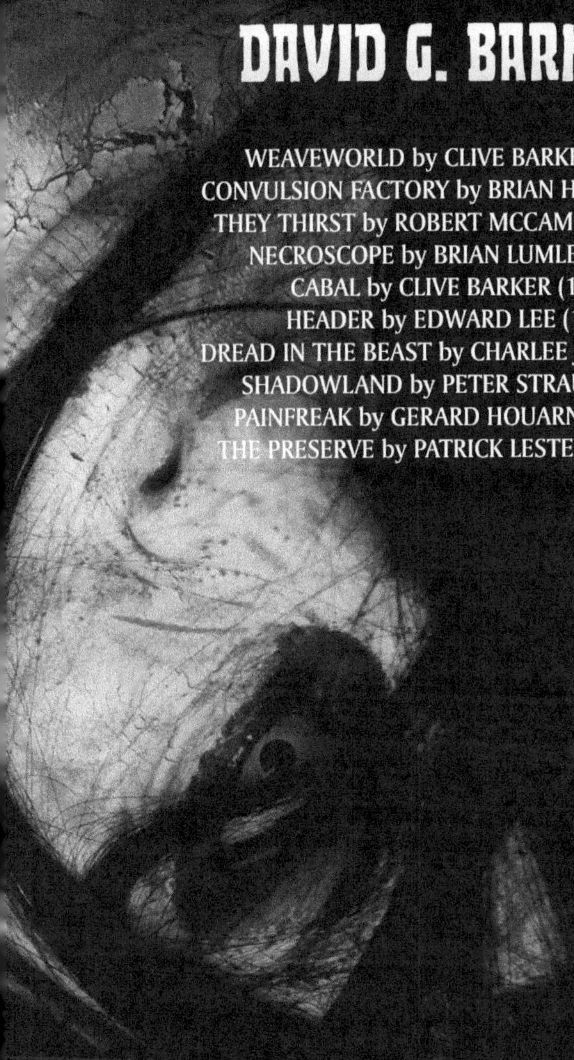

DAVID G. BARNETT was an American writer and editor, and the owner of Necro Publications, an American press specializing in Splatterpunk and hardcore horror fiction. He received the J.F. Gonzalez Lifetime Achievement Award in 2019. He passed away in February 2021, when the Italian edition of this guide was first printed.

EDWARD
LEE
KIKI

THE END?

Not if you want to dive into more of Crystal Lake Publishing's Tales from the Darkest Depths!

Check out our amazing website and online store (https://www.crystallakepub.com)

We always have great new projects and content on the website to dive into, as well as a newsletter, behind the scenes options, social media platforms, and our own dark fiction shared-world series and our very own store. If you use the IGotMyCLPBook! coupon code in the store (at the checkout), you'll get a one-time-only 50% discount on your first eBook purchase!

Our webstore even has categories specifically for KU books, non-fiction, anthologies, novels and novellas.

Alessandro Manzetti

About the Author

About the Editor

Alessandro Manzetti Alessandro Manzetti is a two-time Bram Stoker Award-winning author, editor, scriptwriter and essayist of horror fiction and dark poetry. His work has been published extensively (more than 40 books) in Italian and English, including novels, short and long fiction, poetry, essays, graphic novels and collections.

English publications include his novels *Shanti-The Sadist Heaven* (2019) and *Naraka-The Ultimate Human Breeding* (2018), the novella *The Keeper of Chernobyl* (2019), the collections *The Radioactive Bride* (2020) and *The Garden of Delight* (2017) the poetry collections *Whitechapel Rhapsody* (2020), *The Place of Broken Things* (2019, with Linda D. Addison), *War* (2018, with Marge Simon), *No Mercy* (2017), *Sacrificial Nights* (2016, with Bruce Boston) *Eden Underground* (2015), *Venus Intervention* (2014, with Corrine de Winter), and the graphic novels *Calcutta Horror* (2019), *Her Life Matters* (2020) and *The Horror at Red Hook* (2021)

He edited the anthologies *The Beauty of Death* (2016), *The Beauty of Death Vol. 2 - Death by Water* (2017, with Jodi Renee Lester), *Monsters of Any Kind* (2018, with Daniele Bonfanti) and *2021 Rhysling Anthology* (2021)

His stories and poems have appeared in Italian, USA, UK, Australian, Russian and Polish magazines such as *Weird Tales Magazine, Dark Moon Digest, Splatterpunk Zine, Disturbed Digest, Space and Time Magazine, Darker Magazine, The Horror Zine, Dark Moon Digest, Illumen, Devolution Z, Hinnom, Recompose, Polu Texni, Nothing's Sacred, Okolica Strachu*, and anthologies such as *The Best Horror of the Year* Vol. 13, *Splatterpunk Forever*, *Best Hardcore Horror of the Year* Vol. 2,

4, 5, 6, *The Big Book of Blasphemy*, *Midnight Under the Big Top*, *Rhysling Anthology* (2015, 2016, 2017, 2018, 2019, 2020, 2021), *HWA Poetry Showcase* Vol. 3 and 4, *The Beauty of Death* Vol. 1 and Vol. 2, *World of Light and Darkness*, *One of Us* and many others.

In addition to the Bram Stoker Award (which he has won twice, and been nominated for 12 times), he is a winner of the SFPA Elgin Award (along with eight nominations), and a winner of the HWA Specialty press Award which he received as the owner and editor-in-chief of Independent Legions Press. He has been nominated multiple times for the Splatterpunk Awards, This Is Horror Awards, Rhysling Awards and Indie Horror Books Awards. He has translated works by Ramsey Campbell, Richard Laymon, Poppy Z. Brite, Edward Lee, Graham Masterton, Gary Braunbeck, Gene O'Neill, Lisa Morton, Lucy Snyder, H. P. Lovecraft, Bram Stoker, Edgar Allan Poe, Aleister Crowley.

Manzetti is the CEO and Founder of Independent Legions Publishing, editor of Molotov Magazine (in Italian), an HWA Active member and a former HWA Board of Trustees member. He has twice served on the Bram Stoker Award Lifetime Achievement Award Jury, and in 2021 he served the Science Fiction Poetry Association as the Rhysling Award Chair.

Website: **www.battiago.com**

SUMMARY

Introduction
A CHOIR OF ILL CHILDREN
by Tom Piccirilli
A COLLAPSE OF HORSES
by Brian Evenson
A HEAD FULL OF GHOSTS
by Paul Tremblay
A NEST OF NIGTHMARE
by Lisa Tuttle
ALL THE FABULOUS BEASTS
by Priya Sharma
ALONE WITH THE HORRORS
by Ramsey Campbell
Best Ten Horror Books
Selected by Grady Hendrix
AMERICAN MORONS
by Glen Hirshberg
ANIMALS
by John Skipp & Craig Spector
APOCALYPSE OF THE DEAD
by John McKinney
AT FEAR'S ALTAR
by Richard Gavin
BELOVED
by Toni Morrison
BIRD BOX
by Josh Malerman
Best Ten Horror Books
Selected by Ramsey Campbell
BLACK BUTTERFLIES
by John Shirley
BLACK LEATHER REQUIRED
by David J. Schow
BLACK WIND
by F. Paul Wilson
BLOOD WILL HAVE IT SEASON
by Joseph S. Pulver Sr.
BOY'S LIFE
by Robert R. McCammon
BURNT BLACK SUN
by Simon Strantzas
Best Ten Horror Books
Selected by Paula Guran
CABAL
by Clive Barker
CARRION COMFORT
by Dan Simmons
CLICKERS
by J.F. Gonzalez e M. Williams
COFFIN COUNTY
by Gary Braunbeck
COME CLOSER
by Sara Gran
COME FYGURES COME SHADOWES
by Richard Matheson
Best Ten Horror Books
Selected by S.T. Joshi
COYOTE SONGS
by Gabino Iglesias

CROTA
by Owl Goingback
DARK DANCE
by Tanith Lee
DEAD IN THE WEST
by Joe R. Lansdale
DEAD OF NIGHT
by Jonathan Maberry
DEPRAVED
by Bryan Smith
Best Ten Hardcore Horror Books
Selected by Edward Lee
DOCTOR SLEEP
by Stephen King
DRAWING BLOOD
by Poppy Z. Brite
DREAD IN THE BEAST
by Charlee Jacob
DWELLER
by Jeff Strand
EVERYTHING YOU NEED
by Michael Marshall Smith
EXPERIMENTAL FILM
by Gemma Files
Best Ten Horror Stories
Selected and commented by Stephen Jones
EXQUISITE CORPSE
by Poppy Z. Brite
FEARFUL SYMMETRIES
by Thomas Monteleone
FEVER DREAM
by Samanta Schweblin
FIEND
by Peter Stenson
FLEDGLING
by Octavia E. Butler
FRANKENSTEIN IN BAGHDAD
by Ahmed Saadawi
Best Ten Horror Books
Selected by Brian Evenson
GENERATION LOSS
by Elizabeth Hand
GHOST SUMMER
by Tananarive Due
GONE TO SEETHE RIVER MAN
by Kristophen Triana
GRIMSCRIBE HIS LIVE AND WORKS
by Thomas Ligotti
HADRIANA IN ALL MY DREAMS
by René Depestre
HAIR SIDE, FLESH SIDE
by Helen Marshall
Best Ten Horror Anthologies
Selected by Eric J. Guignard
HAUNTED
by Chuck Palahniuk
HEADER 2
by Edward Lee

HER BODY AND OTHER PARTIES
by Carmen Maria Machado
HOUSE OF LEAVES
by Mark Z. Danielewski
HOUSES WITHOUT DOORS
by Peter Straub
IN SILENT GRAVES
by Gary A. Braunbeck
Best Ten Horror Books
Selected by Owl Goingback
INK
by Jonathan Maberry
ISLAND
by Richard Laymon
IT
by Stephen King
JOHN DIED AT THE END
by David Wong
KIN
by Kealan Patrick Burke
LADY BITS
by Kate Jonez
Best Ten Horror Books
Selected by John Skipp
LET THE RIGHT ONE IN
by John A. Lindqvist
MEXICAN GOTHIC
by Silvia Moreno-Garcia
MISERY
by Stephen King
MISTER SUICIDE
by Nicole Cushing
MY EARLY CRIMES
by Paolo Di Orazio
MOON ON THE WATER
by Mort Castle
NIGHT IN THE LONESOME OCTOBER
by Richard Laymon
Best Ten Horror Books
Selected by Ellen Datlow
NIGHT STONE
by Rick Hautala
NORTH AMERICAN LAKE MONSTERS
by Nathan Ballingrud
NOS4A2
by Joe Hill
OCCULTATION AND OTHER STORIES
by Laird Barron
ODD THOMAS
by Dean Koontz
OFFSPRING
by Jack Ketchum
Best Ten Horror Books
Selected by Steve Rasnic Tem
ONE FOR THE ROAD
by Wesley Southard
OUT OF WATER
by Sarah Read
PANDEMONIUM
by Daryl Gregory

PEACEABLE KINGDOM
by Jack Ketchum
PRETTY LITTLE DEAD GIRLS
by Mercedes Murdock Yardley
REINCARNAGE
by Ryan Harding
Best Ten Horror Essays
Selected and commented by Lisa Morton
REMEMBER WHY YOU FEAR ME
by Robert Shearman
RITUAL
by Graham Masterton
SCARS AND OTHER DISTINGUISHING MARKS
by Richard Christian Matheson
SKIDDING INTO OBLIVION
by Brian Hodge
SKIN
by Kathe Koja
SLOB
by Rex Miller
Best Ten Horror Stories
Selected by Richard Christian Matheson
SOFT APOCALYPSES
by Lucy A. Snyder
SONG FOR THE UNRAVELING OF THE WORLD
by Brian Evenson
SOURDOUGH AND OTHER STORIES
by Angela Slatter
SUFFER THE FLESH
by Monica J. O'Rourke
SURVIVOR
by J.F. Gonzalez
SWAN SONG
by Robert R. McCammon
Best ten Horror Books
Selected by David J. Schow
TASTE OF TENDERLOIN
by Gene O'Neill
THE BRIDGE
by John Skipp & Craig Spector
THE CARP-FACED BOY AND OTHER TALES
by Thersa Matsuura
THE CHANGELING
by Victor LaValle
THE COLLECTION
by Bentley Little
Best Horror Stories of Space and Time
Selected by Angela Yuriko Smith
THE CONQUEROR WORMS
by Brian Keene
THE DEATH ARTIST
by Dennis Etchison
THE DEVIL IN GRAY
by Graham Masterton
THE DIVINITY STUDENT
by Michael Cisco
THE DROWNING GIRL
di Caitlín R. Kiernan

Best Ten Splatterpunk Books
Selected by Jack Bantry
THE DRIVE IN
by Joe R. Lansdale
THE END OF THE END OF EVERYTHING
by Dale Bailey
THE FERRYMAN
by Christopher Golden
THE FINAL RECONCILIATION
by Todd Keisling
THE FISHERMAN
by John Langan
THE GENTLING BOX
by Lisa Mannetti
Best Ten Horror Books
Selected by Joe R. Lansdale
THE GIRL NEXT DOOR
by Jack Ketchum
THE GOLDEN
by Lucius Shepard
THE HELLBOUND HEART
by Clive Barker
THE HOUSE ON NAZARETH HILL
by Ramsey Campbell
THE HUNGER
by Alma Katsu
THE JIGSAW MAN
by Gord Rollo
Best Ten Vampire Books
Selected by Dacre Stoker
THE LESSER DEAD
by Christopher Buehlman
THE LIGHT AT THE END
by John Skipp & Craig Spector
THE LITTLE STRANGER
by Sarah Waters
THE MAN ON THE CEILING
by Steve Rasnic Tem & Melanie Tem
THE MEMORY TREE
by John Little
THE MOUTH OF THE DARK
by Tim Waggoner
Best Ten Horror Books by Black Writers
Selected by Linda D. Addison
THE NIGHT SILVER RIVER RUN RED
by Christine Morgan
THE NIGHTRUNNERS
by Joe R. Lansdale
THE ONES THAT GOT AWAY
by Stephen Graham Jones
THE ONLY GOOD INDIANS
by Stephen Graham Jones
Best Ten Horror Books
Selected by Mort Castle
THE PALE WHITE
by Chad Lutzke
THE RAIN DANCERS
by Greg F. Gifune

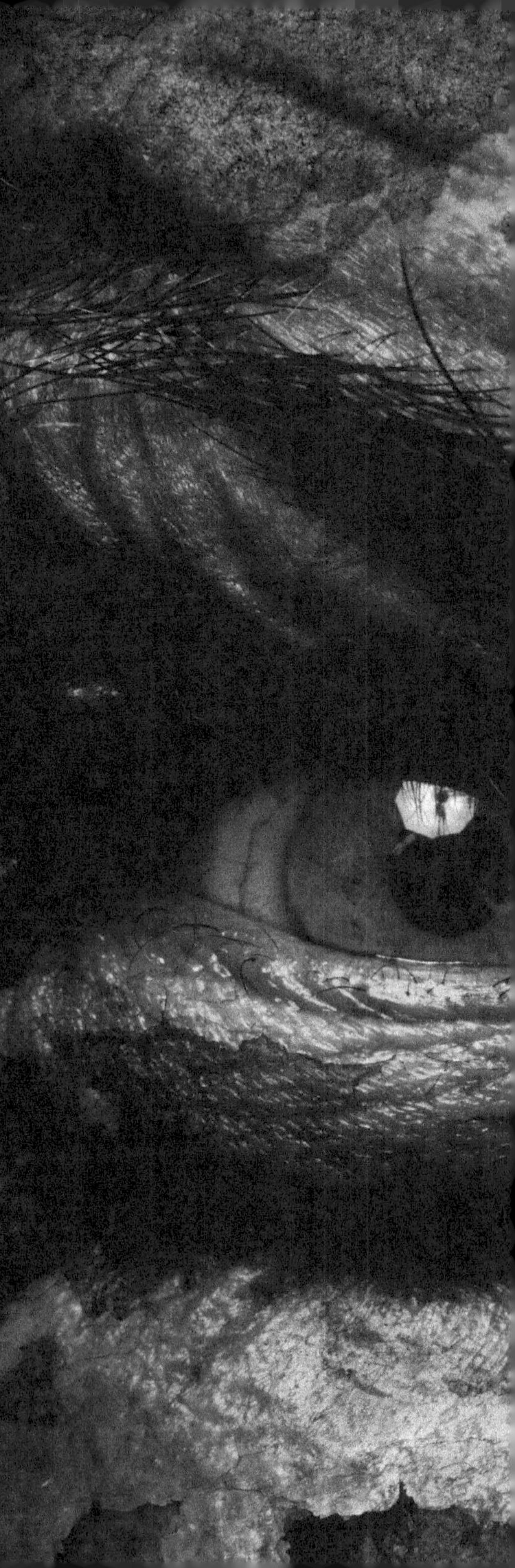

Best Ten Hardcore Horror Books
Selected by Randy Chandler
THE RED TREE
by Caitlín R. Kiernan
THE RESURRECTIONIST
by Wrath James White
THE RISING
by Brian Keene
THE RITUAL
by Adam Nevill
THE RUINS
by Scott Smith
THE RUST MAIDENS
by Gwendolyn Kiste
Best Ten Horror Books
Selected by Lucy Taylor
THE SAFETY OF UNKNOWN CITIES
by Lucy Taylor
THE SHAFT
by David J. Schow
THE SILENCE
by Tim Lebbon
THE SIREN AND THE SPECTER
by Jonathan Janz
THE SOUTHERN BOOK'S CLUB GUIDE
TO SLAYING VAMPIRES
by Grady Hendrix
THE TANK
Nicola Lombardi
THE TERROR
by Dan Simmons
Best Ten Horror Books
Selected by Kate Jonez
THE THROAT
by Peter Straub
THE TRAVELING VAMPIRE SHOW
by Richard Laymon
THE WORST IS YET TO COME
by S.P. Miskowski
THINGS WE LOST IN THE FIRE
by Mariana Enríquez
THIS SYMBIOTIC FASCINATION
by Charlee Jacob
THROUGH A MIRROR, DARKLY
by Kevin Lucia
Best Ten Dark Poetry Collection
Selected by Linda D. Addison
UMBRÍA
by Santiago Eximeno
UNAMERICA
by Cody Goodfellow
WHEN THEY CAME BACK
by Christopher Conlon
Best Ten Horror Books
Selected by Craig Spector
WHITE TRASH GOTHIC
by Edward Lee
WORMWOOD
by Poppy Z. Brite
ZOOPRAXIS
by Richard Christian Matheson
Best Ten Hardcore Horror Books
Selected by David G. Barnett

Readers . . .

It makes our day to know you reached the end of our book. Thank you so much. This is why we do what we do every single day.

Whether you found the book good or great, we'd love to hear what you thought. Please take a moment to leave a short review on Amazon, Goodreads, etc. No need to write an in-depth discussion. Even a single sentence will be greatly appreciated. Reviews go a long way to helping a book sell, and is great for an author's career. It'll also help us to continue publishing quality books. You can also share a photo of yourself holding this book with the hashtag #IGotMyCLPBook!

Thank you again for taking the time to journey with Crystal Lake Publishing.

Visit our Linktree page for a list of our social media platforms. https://linktr.ee/CrystalLakePublishing

Our Mission Statement:

Since its founding in August 2012, Crystal Lake Publishing has quickly become one of the world's leading publishers of Dark Fiction and Horror books in print, eBook, and audio formats.

While we strive to present only the highest quality fiction and entertainment, we also endeavour to support authors along their writing journey. We offer our time and experience in non-fiction projects, as well as author mentoring and services, at competitive prices.

With several Bram Stoker Award wins and many other wins and nominations (including the HWA's Specialty Press Award), Crystal Lake Publishing puts integrity, honor, and respect at the forefront of our publishing operations.

We strive for each book and outreach program we spearhead to not only entertain and touch or comment on issues that affect our readers, but also to strengthen and support the Dark Fiction field and its authors.

Not only do we find and publish authors we believe are

destined for greatness, but we strive to work with men and woman who endeavour to be decent human beings who care more for others than themselves, while still being hard working, driven, and passionate artists and storytellers.

Crystal Lake Publishing is and will always be a beacon of what passion and dedication, combined with overwhelming teamwork and respect, can accomplish. We endeavour to know each and every one of our readers, while building personal relationships with our authors, reviewers, bloggers, podcasters, bookstores, and libraries.

We will be as trustworthy, forthright, and transparent as any business can be, while also keeping most of the headaches away from our authors, since it's our job to solve the problems so they can stay in a creative mind. Which of course also means paying our authors.

We do not just publish books, we present to you worlds within your world, doors within your mind, from talented authors who sacrifice so much for a moment of your time.

There are some amazing small presses out there, and through collaboration and open forums we will continue to support other presses in the goal of helping authors and showing the world what quality small presses are capable of accomplishing. No one wins when a small press goes down, so we will always be there to support hardworking, legitimate presses and their authors. We don't see Crystal Lake as the best press out there, but we will always strive to be the best, strive to be the most interactive and grateful, and even blessed press around. No matter what happens over time, we will also take our mission very seriously while appreciating where we are and enjoying the journey.

What do we offer our authors that they can't do for themselves through self-publishing?

We are big supporters of self-publishing (especially hybrid publishing), if done with care, patience, and planning. However, not every author has the time or inclination to do market research, advertise, and set up book launch strategies. Although a lot of authors are successful in doing it all, strong small presses will always be there for the authors who just want to do what they do best: write.

What we offer is experience, industry knowledge, contacts and trust built up over years. And due to our strong brand and trusting fanbase, every Crystal Lake Publishing book comes with weight of respect. In time our fans begin to trust our judgment and will try a new author purely based on our support of said author.

With each launch we strive to fine-tune our approach, learn from our mistakes, and increase our reach. We continue to assure our authors that we're here for them and that we'll carry the weight of the launch and dealing with third parties while they focus on their strengths—be it writing, interviews, blogs, signings, etc.

We also offer several mentoring packages to authors that include knowledge and skills they can use in both traditional and self-publishing endeavours.

We look forward to launching many new careers.

This is what we believe in. What we stand for. This will be our legacy.

Welcome to Crystal Lake Publishing—
Tales from the Darkest Depths.

www.ingramcontent.com/pod-product-compliance
Lightning Source LLC
Chambersburg PA
CBHW061208210726
48294CB00006B/1789